AF541996

HAUNTED PLACES OF INDIA

{356}

HAUNTED PLACES OF INDIA

Riksundar Banerjee

ALEPH BOOK COMPANY
An independent publishing firm
promoted by ***Rupa Publications India***

First published in India in 2023
by Aleph Book Company
7/16 Ansari Road, Daryaganj
New Delhi 110 002

ISBN: 978-93-93852-25-0

1 3 5 7 9 10 8 6 4 2

Printed in India

CONTENTS

INTRODUCTION

'Hello? Anybody there?', asked a lone traveller, knocking on the door of an abandoned house. The door was covered in weeds. Nobody had visited this house in a long time. Was there something jamming the door? The house was clearly abandoned, but could there be a spirit waiting behind the door? Ghosts and spirits cannot return to the time they came from, but they often leave an impression on the present. Time does not wait for anyone, however, and in various abandoned houses, historical sites, office buildings, and public spaces such as railway stations, traces of a tragic past can suddenly appear and startle everyone. Remnants of a bloody history can lend an uncanny atmosphere to a place.

While the debate on whether or not ghosts exist will continue forever, there is no doubt on the existence of ghostliness. Ghostliness indicates an aura of fear. Every person's fears are unique. Some people are scared of ghost stories they heard in their childhood and others are afraid of writing an exam. A person's socio-economic context, their experiences growing up, and various other factors combined determine who and what they fear. Among many fears of the unknown, the fear of death appears to be the most prevalent. Where do people go after death? Is there any part of the dead that remains? Do people cease to exist when they die? Can someone return from the dead? Questions such as these have forever prevailed in human minds.

In a sense, the past is just frozen time which keeps returning to haunt the present. It reminds us about the history of that time, and if we were to listen carefully, we would have much to learn from. The rich history of India consists of the rise and fall of many empires, attacks from foreign invaders, centuries of colonialism, and various revolutions. With every gory chapter of history, the list of haunted places of the country has grown. The places that witness bloody events in the past become a living memoir of that time. Among these, the Bhulbhulaiya in Lucknow and Bhangarh fort in Rajasthan are popular. This book carefully avoids repeating the elaborate descriptions of these famous places. Lesser-known places such as the Shaniwar Wada fort, Talbehat fort, and the tales surrounding these places are among the stories I have explored in this book.

Every haunted place is unique. The Medical College in Kolkata and the hospital in Manipur have medical incidents that led to death associated with them; Kolkata's National Library and High Court are reminiscent of British rule; the story of Tunnel Number 33 in Shimla looks back on the development of the British Indian Railway. Hahim, Kuldhara village, and Nohkalikai falls are among the places where nature and history blend to create an eerie atmosphere. Some movie theaters and hotels also house terror within their walls. The experiences from Victory Theatre and the Hotel on the Hill could never have a rational explanation. Stories addressing these places have become popular through word of mouth.

The word 'abandoned' also strikes an element of fear. The difference between 'nobody stays there anymore' and 'nobody could stay there' could send a shiver down the spine. The Avadh Palace, the Bonacaud Bungalow are some places like this, where past incidents linger beyond closed doors and create a fear of the unknown. In the eeriness of such locations, one can get a glimpse of the past if observed closely enough. Empty campuses like Madras Christian College also have an uncanny atmosphere at night. Lonely highways and roads like NH-33 or Hoskote Road are often the site of supernatural encounters. The uneasy feeling around crematoriums and graveyards is the subject of the story of Kalpalli.

This book tries to explore how fear spreads among the groups of people around a specific location. Behind many of the fears, there exist tragic historical events and these incidents showcase the dark side of human nature. For this book, I have collected legends, facts, and oral tales from various sources. I personally visited some of these sites. With the passage of time, the notion of fear has increased at some places and been completely vanquished at some. After reading this book, if someone pauses for a moment at any of these places and wonders what might be going on beyond what our senses can comprehend, I would consider my efforts fruitful.

Riksundar Banerjee
Kolkata
August 2022

1
THE TRAFFIC SERGEANT AT HASTINGS

There are many stories about the ever-changing nights of Kolkata. The crossroads at Hastings, the turn around the P. G. Hospital—these are places that a streaming river of people pass by every day. But a few decades ago, these streets were not as crowded. The call-a-cab apps were yet to be invented; yellow taxis ruled the streets. And at times, solitude was the only company around these long, wide roads. The lonely street lights, standing vigilant, guarding the city from darkness, are the only witnesses to the changes that have taken place over time.

This is a story from a couple of decades ago. Madhab was waiting at the crossroads at Hastings in his yellow cab. It was going to be hard to find a passenger there at night. He was tired from a long day and would have liked some company on his way back home. Waiting in his cab, Madhab was falling in and out of sleep. With the insouciance of the night, having no care at home and the little hope that someone may still come around looking for a cab, it was a still night; water calmly flowed under the Howrah bridge. A bunch of dogs were quarrelling amongst themselves over some food packets. Suddenly, he awoke to a gentle knock on the back door of his car.

Madhab was used to people knocking on the front door and negotiating the fare through the window before they got on board. Another set of knocks shook him out of his thoughts. Madhab sat upright and looked at the back, 'Who's there?'

'Bhowanipur Police Station?'

A cop was standing there in a traffic sergeant's uniform. His shift had probably just ended and he resorted to taking a cab instead of waiting for the police car. This was far from ideal. Police officers were not the kind of passengers one desired at night. They often had no fixed destination and bargained a lot before paying. But before Madhab could say a word, the sergeant had already opened the door and sat on the backseat. Tall, healthy body, bright skin in a neat uniform. Though he must've been returning home from his duty, there was no sign of fatigue nor any sign of wear on his uniform. Looking at him in the rear-view mirror, Madhab figured that this person was in no mood to talk. He was looking out the window from the backseat. The weather was a little cooler now with the wind blowing and the roads pretty much empty. Bhowanipur Police Station would not be a long ride. The sergeant had probably fallen asleep in the light breeze.

There were not many red lights on the way, just one more turn and the destination will be short drive away. It would be all good if he pays right. Madhab couldn't even demand extra money from a police officer just because it was late. His eyes casually rolled over the looking glass, and then again. There was nobody in the back! Where did the sergeant go? Madhab parked the cab on the roadside and looked back—there was nobody there. He got out of the car, opened the back door and checked again, but couldn't find anyone there. Did that guy just vanish into thin air? The cab never stopped for long. It was impossible to get down from a running car without him noticing it. He turned around and drove back on the road he had just come along, but he did not find a single wandering soul. The only presence was the strange mystery of the light and shadows.

A few days later, Saptarshi was driving home around the Hastings crossroads. The road was empty and he planned to reach home fast while humming to music. He was about to take the turn when a traffic sergeant waved his hand. He was probably trying to collect a bribe. Saptarshi had all his papers in the car, there was no way that guy could get him to take out some money. He stopped the car. The constable silently went near the rear door.

'Lift...Bhowanipur Police Station.'

This was an unexpected turn of events. He considered whether he ought to offer a lift to a stranger at this late hour.

It could be someone in a fake uniform, trying to scam him. He snapped out of his thoughts when he noticed that the guy had already boarded his car. He was certain that the door was locked, how did he get in? If dropping him off to Bhowanipur Police Station would do it, so be it, he thought as he started the car. It won't take long but having a complete stranger in the backseat of his car in the middle of the night was making him uncomfortable. He was not used to driving anyone other than his family members and a few friends. He frequently glanced at the stranger in the rear-view mirror. A few minutes later, there was a sudden jerk. Saptarshi looked at the back seat. There was nobody there anymore. How was that possible? He had been driving fairly fast, how could someone get off the car? He stopped and looked around, but there was nobody to be seen.

A few months passed by. That incident at Hastings had faded from Madhab's memory. It was a rainy night. Madhab's cab was once again at those crossroads. The wipers were noisily clearing the windshield. The heavy rain and the yellow light from the street lights together created an eerie atmosphere. Was there someone at the roadside? Madhab slowed down the car and saw a person in a traffic police uniform, struggling on the ground, with one hand raised. Getting closer, Madhab was shocked to recognize a familiar face. It was the sergeant who took his cab a few months back, towards the police station of Bhowanipur! His forehead was covered in blood and even more was flowing down his face. His white uniform had turned red. Madhab stopped the car to get the person to the nearest hospital. But just as he stepped out, the sergeant disappeared. Madhab could hear him wailing but the sound was faint, the rainwater puddle at that spot was still red from the blood. Where did he vanish? He was in his cab that day, and lay injured by the roadside just a moment ago. How had he just disappeared?

Madhab could not sleep that night. Whenever he tried to close his eyes, he could hear the wailing of that constable from Hastings and his blood-covered face flashed before his eyes. He was asking for help to save his life, and his throat craved for a little water while the rain washed away the blood from his body, the begging for help with one feebly raised arm. Madhab felt terribly guilty. He could not do anything to help that poor fellow. He had brushed off the first incident but what he saw that night was unnatural.

Madhab started out in his cab at first light. There weren't many shops around this side of the town but there was a tea stall on his way from South Kolkata. He parked the cab and stopped there. Many mysteries come to light when the sun rises. The morning's crowd was slowly beginning to show, the city was creeping out of its slumber with the rising sun. Madhab asked the tea stall owner if there had been an accident around the corner the previous night. That man stood still for a couple of moments and asked, 'Did you see a traffic policeman?'

'Yeah, last night, just a little way back…'

'Did you go near him?'

'Yes! I approached him to see if I could help him in any

way. But as soon as I stepped out, he vanished!'

'The one you saw is not a human. He passed away, right there, long ago.'

'What do you mean?'

'It was right before his shift ended at night, he was hit by a truck and collapsed by the roadside. Nobody came to help. One after the other cars passed by but none of them stopped to help. Not a single one of us knew about the incident and the poor fellow bled to death, right there.'

'But he was in my cab, and then by the road from last night.... Why would I happen to be the one seeing him?'

'Some people can see him, asking for lift at night, and then he vanishes on the way. Some people can see him begging for help at the crossroads. I have never seen him even though I stayed this close for many years. A lot of us don't even know about the accident.'

Madhab felt remorseful. The first time he saw the sergeant, he had suspected whether the guy was a police officer in the first place. Such an awful incident—how bad was the fate of this person who was responsibile for the safety of others. Nobody even spared a drop of water for him. Madhab walked to that spot, the road had dried from last night's rain and there was no trace of blood.

When driving by the crossroads at Hastings at night, if a police officer asks for a lift or some help—it won't hurt to stop a little. Even though he is lost forever, he returns to that place every once in a while to see if some human with a conscience will help him.

2

THE LITTLE GIRL FROM PUNE

From the legends that live on for decades, to gossip exchanged over evening tea breaks, it's the stories that keep a city alive. Pune is one of the most attractive cities in the state of Maharashtra. With a rich history and a growing population, there are many stories to unfurl in Pune. Places such as the Bhaje and Karla Buddhist Caves and the Sinhagad fort attract thousands of tourists to the city, while new industries and the market for jobs attract those seeking new opportunities. But some haunting stories creep in the shadows of this glowing, beautiful, high-tech city.

One of the ominous places that is feared by the locals is Chandannagar. Not many people are concerned about this area during the day but those who have heard its tales are cautious about venturing out there at night. The big buildings at Chandannagar cast long shadows across the roads on a moonlit night and sudden sounds from construction often startle people. And if they spot a lonely little girl playing with a doll at late hours in this area, they have to be extremely careful.

Suresh had heard such a story long before he was deputed as a night guard at the Blue Paradise Resort. He was warned not to take a single step forward if he spotted a kid while running an errand or on his evening walk. But with the preoccupations of his new job, the warning had slipped to the back of his mind. One night, he was closing the entry gate after one of the apartment residents drove in with their car and he spotted a little girl, wearing a frock, sitting in a shadowy corner across the street. She seemed to be staring at something in her lap. Had the girl run away from home? Suresh became concerned and approached to help her. When he crossed the street, the girl was not there. He looked around and found her on the stairs outside another house. Wondering how the girl ran away so fast, he started walking in her direction but the girl vanished from that spot too. All those stories of Chandannagar flashed back into Suresh's mind. Could those stories be true? Was that little girl he saw a person from the past? Was she some kind of ghost?

Suresh grew alert of his surroundings. He kept looking around as he slowly walked back to the gate. Suddenly, he heard laughter. It was the laugh of a little girl but he could not make out the source of the sound. When the laughter stopped, he heard a strange, monotonous sobbing. It sounded like the suppressed crying of a child who was hurt. The sound seemed to come from the construction site at first but later it could also be heard from the corner of the street ahead. Some faint memory cautioned him from taking a step in either direction.

Numbed with fear and confusion, Suresh turned around to find girl standing right in front of him. She had a look of revenge and anger in her eyes. The doll she held had its head torn off its torso. Suddenly a car approached the street and the kid vanished into thin air. Suresh felt the strength return to his body and ran back to his post as fast as he could.

A few years ago, one of the residents of Chandannagar was driving home on a windy night. The road was empty, his home was not far, and the surroundings were well-lit. As he drove forward, he thought he saw a little girl standing in the middle of the road. What was she doing there in the middle of the night? Suddenly, the girl started sprinting towards his car. He pulled himself together and managed to push the brakes in time. It would be fatal if she got hit by the car! When the car came to a halt, there was nobody around. Everything was silent except the sound of a little girl crying, seemingly coming from under his car. Shivering in fear, he tried to restart his car, but the engine did not cooperate. He looked at his phone. There was no network coverage. He tried to get out of the car but he could not unlock the doors. He was full of dread. As the crying continued, he could not comprehend how long it had been and he felt like he was about to die right there. It took him a long time to calm down. Finally, after a few cars passed him by, he unlocked the door and got out of the car. The girl was nowhere to be found.

This incident left him scarred. Every time he was behind the wheel at night, he could see that little girl standing right in front of him. He avoided driving at night altogether.

Supernatural experiences like these are widely shared. They are told and retold in vivid detail by so many people that it starts to seem like a greater number of people have had such an encounter. Pune locals report hearing suppressed sobbing and a child's laughter around Chandannagar and none recall the source of those sounds.

Life is fast in this city, but events like these live on in the consciousness of people. Even though the streets are well-lit, people stay alert when walking through them at night. Fear lingers in places like Chandannagar.

Remember this story when you visit the beautiful city of Pune. You may see a little girl crying alone at a street corner. A girl whose life came to an end like a flower that was plucked right before it bloomed. Maybe she died in a construction accident decades ago. Some say she is still trying to find her way back home.

3

THE HOSPITAL IN IMPHAL

The capital of Manipur is one of a kind. It has maintained its uniqueness in spite of adapting to the constant modernization. The state of Manipur, surrounded by mountains, has an awe-inspiring natural beauty and a rich history, but it is also a region that has known its share of conflict. When one approaches the locals to ask about the urban legends and horror stories, these people would give them a reality check. They are so concerned with the daily struggle for survival in this environment and the things that they need to be fearful of, that fear of ghosts and supernatural entities would be a luxury.

Imphal's haunted destinations lie at the very heart of the city. The stories of these places are interwoven with the mundane daily lives of the city's residents. The local history and geography play a significant role in the formation of the spooky stories related to any place. Urban legends and stories of hauntings set in modern times are spookier than stories of a forgotten past or the bygone era of kings and queens. One such story that roams around Imphal does not feature ancient ruins or abandoned forts, but a government hospital that was constructed in 1989 to serve the common people. The hospital is an active, busy institution catering to hundreds of people every day, many whose lives are on the verge of death.

The hospital is situated in East Imphal. It boasts of advanced treatment facilities but if anybody asks about the safety of the restrooms and corridors around the female ward, both hospital staff and locals would provide a mixed, hesitant response. A lot of them have not experienced anything first-hand but they strongly believe that something exists in those places. Apart from the patients, visiting family members have also had some strange encounters in this hospital. One explanation is that every hospital witnesses several births and deaths on a daily basis. It is easy for someone to associate supernatural elements with these events. Hundreds of people return from the hospital with their hearts filled with joy or grief, and their heightened emotional state can make them see or hear something that does not exist. The hospital makes no mention of anything even distantly related to this, but some curious minds have kept the tales and other people's experiences alive for years. The story of this hospital in East Imphal is somewhat different from any other story of a haunted hospital.

'A guy came to visit his wife one afternoon…something

happened to him…' said the nurse. 'He was determined to move his wife to some other hospital. Every time someone asked him for a reason, he would say he experienced something strange and unnatural. Whenever he was walking down the corridor, he had a strange feeling of being followed but the moment he turned back, there was nobody behind him. When he entered the restroom, he felt the presence of another person but there was nobody there other than him. Then as he was leaving the ward with this uneasy feeling, someone walked past him and giggled in his ear. The guy could not see anybody around and he was scared out of his wits. For their safety, he decided to have his wife admitted to a different hospital.'

One of the janitors at the hospital had a similar story to tell. He, too, felt the presence of some invisible beings. He heard heavy breathing, he even felt a warm breath on his shoulder when he was cleaning the corridors and the restrooms alone in the morning or at night. Relying on the hospital for his livelihood, he could not leave the place as easily as the other guy.

The stories of sightings and strange experiences are not for the faint-hearted, who would feel a chill down their spine if they were to visit this place. A twenty-year-old visited this hospital, purely out of curiosity, after listening to the rumours. He was a science student and he was convinced that he could debunk the myth about the hospital. He didn't find anything unnatural about the restroom and the haunted corridor. A patient's relative had told him that she felt a chill on her way back from the restroom. It was in the peak of summer but the change in temperature could be attributed to the cross-ventilation in that narrow corridor. However, the chill persisted the entire time she was there. She was not sick and the moment they came out of that corridor, everything instantly felt normal.

It is impossible to settle the debate between facts and rumours in this case. Once the name of this hospital came to be associated with supernatural incidents the idea spread among a large number of people. While the hospital is not too old, the number of reported incidents are.

If you visit Manipur, you can take an evening walk around this hospital. And if you suddenly feel someone whispering in your ear or heavy breathing on your shoulder, you may ask yourself, 'Did I just experience that? Is someone else here?'

4

TARBAHAR RAILWAY CROSSING

When studying the locations where some kind of supernatural activity is said to have taken place, we find that they have a history associated with them. There is usually an incident that has left a mark on the people residing in the neighbourhood and cast a blanket of fear around the site. Many public spaces witness tragic or violent incidents. This is why even places that are buzzing with activity can have a shadow of horror that lurks beneath their everyday appearance. In mapping horror hotspots across India, we have come across places that are fairly popular. The Tarbahar railway crossing, located in Chattisgarh's Bilaspur, is a recent addition to this list of haunted places.

A deadly accident at the railway crossing at Tarbahar has had a strong effect on its surroundings. An eeriness is palpable at this spot even though nothing supernatural has been reported so far. The accident took place in 2011 when thirteen people from an adjoining slum lost their lives at the crossing. The residents of the slum regularly crossed the railtracks, which were usually used by slow-moving wagon carriers, to get to the other side of the road. On the day of the accident a big group was crossing the tracks, they had seen two wagon carriers in the distance and thought they would be able to cross before the trains came close. Just at that time, a super-fast passenger train came through the middle track. In the blink of an eye, thirteen people lost their lives and a lot more were severely injured. The granite and fishplates were covered in blood and flesh. The entire slum burst into cries and the wailings of people who had lost their loved ones in this brutal accident could be heard for days. The locals believe that the unfortunate group of people who died that day still keep walking across the railtracks.

This nondescript railway crossing became known overnight because of the accident. The tragedy caused a general outcry and after an investigation, a compensation was provided to the families. People pray before stepping closer to the Tarbahar railway crossing at night. The horror of this occurrence and the effect it had on people has made people more vigilant while crossing the tracks.

Many locals refuse to cross the tracks at Tarbahar because they believe that the souls of the dead people disturb the living ones while they try to cross. The wandering spirits try to confuse people and try to trap them into making the same mistake they did and cause another accident.

There is another tale, a rather strange one, roaming around this place. Though there is no eyewitness to this incident, there are plenty of residents eager to describe it elaborately. It was late into the night. A few people were heading to the crossing. They looked at the tracks, there was nothing to be seen in either direction. Suddenly, as they started walking, a train's horn became audible from the middle track. The train sped past them and, to their great surprise, those men were completely unharmed. The next moment, they disappeared into thin air. Since then, people have believed that the victims of the accident in 2011 still linger around the railway crossing. If any living person meets them on their way, that person would have to encounter mortal danger. The slum dwellers can hear noises from tracks in the dead of the night, some identify those noises as the helpless screams of a human caught in grave danger.

Another story the locals narrate can't be exactly marked as a ghost story or a real incident; rather, it is a version of a gory episode from the history of this place. The story is about a young boy who was about to cross the railtracks at Tarbahar. When he was about to take a step, he saw a man from the other side waving at him, indicating that he should stop and not cross the lines. The boy stopped, but the man he saw was walking towards the track as a fast-moving train appeared out of nowhere. When the man reached too close to the train, the boy screamed in fear. Right then, the sound of train engine drowned all other noises in the surroundings. The scream was lost in the noise of the passing train. When the train left, the baffled boy saw that the guy who was just run over was slowly walking again. His entire body was covered in blood but there was a smirk on the face. The boy turned around and ran for his life.

The aura of fear that enters the minds of people after a violent, gory incident keeps morphing into different forms over time. It keeps the memory of such accidents alive and also reminds people of the precautions they should take.

The Tarbahar railway crossing accident has marked the spot as a place of horror. Maybe, like Chhattisgarh's Tarbahar, someone may witness a group of souls walking across railtracks elsewhere, a group who could never reach the other side of the railway crossing.

5

JHARKHAND'S NH-33

National Highway 33 stretches from Arwal to Farakka, connecting Bihar and West Bengal. A stretch of this highway is infamous for being one of the most dangerous roads in the country. A story of terror covers this part of the highway. A high number of accidents that take place on this stretch cause more injuries than normals, resulting in a high percentage of fatality among the victims. About ten years ago, road accidents took place here nearly every day and almost all of them ended in a death. Fear of this place is so rampant that a lot of people begin their journey with pujas and making offerings at the two temples at either end of this portion of the road. The part we are talking about spans from Bundu to Tamar, this is where the highest number of accidents occur. This naturally raises a lot of questions. The government has promised to repair the highway and broaden that particular stretch, although the exact cause of the road accidents is shrouded in mystery. The people who travel here regularly have many different beliefs as well as some peculiar experiences. Often, a cursed spirit is blamed for the numerous fatalities.

This area was also in the news during the time of Maoist revolutions. The fear of sudden attacks, snatching, and robbery would linger here. In the last three years, however, this place has only been in the news because of the road accidents which have caused over two hundred and fifty deaths. The people travelling from Jamshedpur start their journey only after they have performed puja at the temple of Vaan devi for a safe trip. Similarly, those travelling from the Ranchi end of the highway offer prayers at the Hanuman and Kali temples in Taimara Ghanti before commencing their trip. The priests at the temples and the constables patrolling the route and collecting tolls at the checkposts believe that some kind of evil supernatural power is to be blamed for the loss of so many lives. The investigation of the accidents reveals the fact that most of them happened when drivers lost control of their vehicles. There have been accidents where an entire bus crashed with such severity that none of the passengers survived. A belief about an evil spirit and a ghostly presence on the road features in the local folklore. Many people prefer alternate ways just to avoid this route after daylight. The tales about the highway describe the ghost of a tall woman who roams along the road in the dark. She startles the drivers when they are driving, leading them to their demise.

Who is this tall woman in white? Several people from the nearby area could tell you about this ghost—a tall woman draped in a traditional white saree—and her hauntings on NH-33. According to some, the woman died in a violent car crash and all the members of her family met the same fate in other road accidents. Others speculate that she had to face a slow and painful end, being trapped in a locked car after an accident. There are stories about the ghost appearing on the roadside where the cars go whooshing by. People assume that she is waiting for someone, but suddenly she starts walking to the middle of the road. Accidents happen in the blink of an eye. The drivers push the brakes to save the woman walking in the middle of the road but the cars lose control in an instant, resulting in a deadly accident.

Government authorities have their own logical explanation about the number of accidents happening on this road. According to them, the highway is highly prone to accidents due to a high number of blind turns. They advise the relevant authorities to be stricter about enforcing the speed limits on the way. People who don't believe in the ghost stories have also travelled on this road several times just to demonstrate that nothing out of the ordinary happens here. However, listening to the first-hand experience of someone who escaped death by a hair's breadth really makes a chill run down your spine. The people who avoided a fatal accident describe the same tall, old woman in a white saree appearing in front of their vehicles, only to vanish the next moment. The night travellers have heard the laughs of a woman coming from the blind turns of the road but there has never been a definite source of the sound. These drivers too have understood that being distracted by the laugh and taking their eyes off the road could cause deadly accidents, especially when they are driving at a good speed on an empty highway.

Despite the two temples on the two ends of the highway, it seems like divinity has no power over this road. Those who believe the supernatural stories still worship at these temples, making offerings for the puja before starting their journey on this route. The existence of supernatural power on NH-33 may not be something that can be verified right away, but these stories do contribute significantly to the earnings of these two temples. The fear of danger prompts people to put their faith in divine power.

The locals advise running away if anyone sees a woman draped in a white saree on the highway. She may be asking for help, looking at you with her helpless eyes, but you should not stop there at any cost. And in case the woman jumps in front of the vehicle, you would only reach your destination alive if you can manoeuvre the vehicle quickly enough to get past the old woman. Nobody knows whether that woman too, had somewhere to reach. She does not have an address to return to now. But you do. Your family is here, waiting for you. You have a destination to reach safely. If you happen to be passing through NH-33 at any point, take extra safety measures and keep your speed under control.

6

THE SHANIWAR WADA

The Shaniwar Wada of Pune has seen the sun rise for nearly three hundred years. Housing a number of mahals and magnificent fountains, the fort is an attractive tourist destination. There are five gates to the Shaniwar Wada, namely, Dilli Darwaja, Mastani Darwaja, Khirki Darwaja, Ganesh Darwaja, and Jambhul Darwaja or Narayana Darwaja. However, there is also a gory history associated with this fort which has led to plenty of rumours. A young boy's agonizing screams can be heard from this fort on full-moon nights as he pleads for his life. 'Kaka, mal vachwa!' he screams, appealing to his uncle to save his life. To know who that young boy was and how he came to be in this situation, we need to take a look back at the history of the Shaniwar Wada.

Peshwa Bajirao I laid the foundation stones of the Shaniwar Wada in 1730. The construction began on a Saturday or 'Shaniwar', thus the fort was named Shaniwar Wada. The word 'Wada' means a residential complex in Marathi. Two years after the construction began, on another Saturday, the Peshwa moved here and made it his home. The peshwas were leaders of the Maratha empire. Bajirao I, the seventh peshwa of the Maratha empire ruled for twenty years. He passed away in 1740, and his son, Balaji Bajirao, became the next peshwa. Following this, Shaniwar Wada became the site of internal political conflict and a scramble for power.

Balaji Bajirao had three sons: Madhabrao, Bishwasrao, and Narayanrao. After Balaji Bajirao and his son, Bishwasrao, were killed in the Third Battle of Panipat, the throne was inherited by Madhabrao. However, Madhabrao did not remain peshwa for long. One of the deadliest diseases of the time, tuberculosis, took his life in 1772. After his demise, Balaji Bajirao's last son, Narayanrao inherited the title. Narayanrao was only sixteen years old at the time. This was not welcomed by his uncle, Balaji Bajirao's younger brother, Raghunath Rao and his wife Anandi Bai who wanted to improve her position in the empire. As Raghunath Rao began ruling from the shadows, Anandi Bai wanted the position of peshwani for herself. On the other hand, despite being an underage teenager, Narayanrao did not always accept the advice of his uncle without question. Raghunath could not ignore the lust for power any longer as his wife kept provoking him to take some action to overthrow the peshwa. He teamed up with a powerful clan of hunters, known as the Gardi clan. The main link between Raghunath Rao, Anandi Bai, and the Gardi clan was a servant named Tulaji Pawar. Tulaji had instructions from Anandi Bai to bring Raghunath Rao's letters to her and to deliver them only after she had finished scrutinizing them. Raghunath had promised special privileges to the Gardis if they could succeed in putting Narayanrao in captivity. These secret letters conveying his message to the Gardis came into the hands of Anandi Bai. She was a cunning woman and she thought of eliminating the risk to the power she desired. She changed the directions in the letter, asking the Gardis to kill Narayanrao instead of holding him in captivity.

On the last day of 1773's Ganesh festival, the day of Anant Chaturdashi, when an eighteen-year-old Narayanrao was sleeping peacefully in the afternoon unaware of the conspiracy running against him, the Gardi clan's army attacked the fort. Narayanrao immediately understood the imminent danger to his life. The very family of his uncle's, who were behind the entire conspiracy, were the first ones to come to his mind to seek shelter and safety from the killers. Young Narayanrao rushed towards his uncle, screaming and pleading, 'Kaka! Mala Vachwa!' meaning 'Uncle! Save my life!' but there was nobody to save him. The Gardis killed the young peshwa in the attack that lasted just about half an hour.

The Marathas lost power in the Third Anglo-Maratha war of 1818. Until then, constant internal turmoil for power had permeated Shaniwar Wada. Once, it was home to over a thousand people, but with time, the entire fort was left abandoned. In 1828, a devastating fire caused massive damage to the fort, but its attraction has stood the test of time. The fort still stands tall, having witnessed the rise and fall of an empire, the coming and going of rulers, the conspiracy for the throne, and much more. After the death of the young Peshwa Narayanrao, his spirit kept returning to Shaniwar Wada every full-moon night. The wandering soul continues to ask for help from the very people who wronged him. His screams cut through the silence and darkness of the castle at night.

The young boy may not return to the fort every full moon, but stories about him keep circling the fort. If you visit this fort on your trip to Pune and stand in front of the main gates on a full-moon night, under the shadow of the seven-storeyed fort, you too, might hear these tales or even a young boy's scream. Or perhaps, as with any tales, the rumoured screams could have been created by the people.

7

THE WOMAN AT THE KHOONI NALA

The picturesque state of Jammu and Kashmir is called heaven on earth. With mountains, lakes, and narrow winding roads that cut through the mountains filled with varieties of flowers and leaves, the beauty of Kashmir has attracted tourists for hundreds of years from all over the nation and beyond. In spite of the conflict in the region, Kashmir remains in the bucket list of nature lovers too. Away from the tourist attractions, there are some places in Kashmir that are known for their stories and the experiences associated with them. Many locations in this paradise on earth are feared by people. Some places become famous because of the horror stories associated with them while others fade from the spotlight—both of these types of places can be found in Kashmir. One of these locations deserves a special mention, the Khooni Nala.

The infamous Khooni Nala is located on Jammu–Srinagar National Highway. One side of the winding road is a rough, steep mountain and on the other side, there is a deadly cliff. Being an area that is naturally prone to landslides, nets are set on the mountain bodies so that chunks of rocks don't fall away suddenly. These roads often get blocked by snow during the winter. Tourists often halt at various winding routes to observe the magnificent view, but most of them usually avoid this specific place as it is widely feared. Terrible accidents such as vehicles filled with passengers falling off the cliff have taken place around the Khooni Nala. The drivers take special care here because of their fear of seeing something on the road. It is thought that the stretch right before the Banihal Tunnel was named Khooni Nala because of the many accidents and deaths that took place here. One belief is that the souls of the people who died in the accidents roam around the region and try to haunt other people. Another stronger belief suggests that all of these accidents were caused because of the existence of one specific woman.

This woman is a mysterious character in the story of Khooni Nala. People have reported that while driving on this national highway a woman clad in a black saree appears out of nowhere, standing in the middle of the road, holding a baby in her arms. This apparently harmless woman figure has a horrific story. The woman asks for a lift in the vehicles passing by. If a driver of the car ignores her plea and doesn't allow her to get in the vehicle, they inevitably meet with a horrible road accident, or fall off the cliff, ending in the certain death of every single person onboard. There are lots of questions raised about this woman wearing a black saree. While searching for answers people have found that a pregnant young woman had committed suicide by jumping off the cliff at Khooni Nala a long time ago. Since that time, her spirit keeps coming back, letting others know about her presence in the place. She stops random vehicles on the road and asks for a lift to a nearby place. Most of the vehicles who refuse her request end up in grave danger. Some of the drivers lose control of their cars, and in most cases, the passengers begin feeling sick after a little while and feel like a dark shadow is following their vehicle.

There is another possible outcome of the woman asking for a lift. The drivers who know about the danger of not giving a ride to that woman submit to the plea and take her in. As the car drives on, the woman and her child begin to fade away like a shadow.Those cars or the passengers onboard do not face any accidents during their trip. Many passengers have experienced sudden changes in the temperature inside the car and nausea or headaches while passing that portion of the road.

Amid the mind blowing beauty of Kashmir, there exists this strange, scary place near the Banihal Tunnel, where people must decide whether they should bring their cars to a halt or keep driving when confronted by this strange, unexpected hindrance to their journeys. Even if we ignore the supernatural elements for a moment, if a woman in a black saree holding an infant in her arms asks for a lift by stopping a car on a winding mountain road, we should be alert and cautious.

Khooni Nala's story has become known throughout the country. This story of the suicide of an expecting mother and her return to the mortal world probably hints at the reasons why a woman would be forced to take a step like that. Kashmir has many political issues of its own. Due to this, many horror stories have emerged from the region. It may be the embodiment of heaven on earth, but not everything in this heavenly place is mandated to be beautiful.

8

THE PICNIC AT HAHIM

A few students of the Assam Engineering college had gathered for their usual hangout. They were talking about finding a new place for their next picnic. As winter approached, the excitement about their picnic plans grew and these students were planning their activities in advance. One of them was searching for uncommon picnic spots online and stumbled upon a picnic spot named Hahim. The route to this place was pretty convenient for them and the photographs looked beautiful too, but, with the elaborate description of the place, there were quite a few links to articles mentioning various supernatural incidents that occurred at this location. Hahim picnic spot was labelled as one of the most haunted places in Assam. The hot-blooded engineering students were thrilled after reading all the stories of supernatural activities happening around Hahim. They were discussing whether to pick Hahim as the destination for their winter picnic. The discussion was between a group of five or six students, but the total number of people participating in this picnic would be well over fifty. These five boys knew that the others would not disagree with the location they chose. Shantanu, one of the boys in this group, was unusually silent with a grim expression on his face. Sakshi turned around to ask Shantanu's opinion about this destination. Shantanu paused for a couple of seconds and began sharing the story about the experience his elder brother had had on a trip with friends. When he started sharing the story, a few of these friends had a slight smirk, others were having a different conversation, but as he proceeded with the tale, all of their faces began bearing a completely different expression.

Hahim is located in Assam's Boko. It is a beautiful picnic spot close to forests, mountain streams, and scattered rocks. The highway is nearby. Being a popular picnic spot, it becomes very difficult to find a suitable spot here during the peak season. For Shantanu's brother's group, their government officers had picked Hahim for a outing. Very few of them knew about the supernatural elements attached to the place, and the others did not care about the stories. They dismissed the entire thing, believing that it was nothing but a hoax. A few more picnic parties had gathered on the spot on that beautiful sunny day. Shantanu's brother wandered off from the group, he found a quiet place around the stream where the wet rocks and the moss stuck on those rocks under the water made a beautiful, eye-soothing scene. The stream flowed with a calming sound, little rocks tumbled in the water. Faint noises of people talking, laughing, and playing music were coming from a distance. In this place, the sun was not too hot either. The breeze was fairly cold. With the bright sun above it was a mesmerizing atmosphere.

Quite a bit of time had passed. Among all the noise and excitement, Shantanu's brother's friends noticed that he had been missing for a long time. They thought that he probably went on a walk, away from the noise and the crowd. But as time passed, they got tense and started calling his phone. The cell was out of network coverage. The group now scattered around, looking for their missing friend. There was a large area to cover and the search party could not see any sign of Shantanu's brother. An atmosphere of fear started to build among the members. They had heard some creepy stories about Hahim before arriving there, and even if they did not believe those tales, the negative thoughts at the moment of crisis became overpowering.

Shantanu's brother, like a hypnotized person, was roaming around in that shadowy place where it felt like evening even at noon. He was walking on the lonely road in a strangely calm manner. The weather was slightly cold and soothing. He had completely forgotten why, where, and when he had come to this place. Listening to the birds' chirping and the wind blowing through the leaves of the surrounding trees, his only feeling was to keep moving forward, hoping he would behold something astonishingly beautiful right behind the corner of the road. He felt like the rocks beneath his feet had turned into soft, mushy grass. After a little bit of time, it began to get dark, as if the day had ended and evening was about to fall. Crickets were chirping everywhere, a few stars could be seen in the sky above. Going forward, he saw a lonely woman sitting beside the stream, her head bent down as if she was crying. Naturally, his attention kept diverting to that woman and despite repeatedly thinking of walking away in another direction, his subconscious kept pulling his feet towards that weeping woman. The woman, possibly hearing his footsteps, slowly turned her head towards him. He looked at her again, the face had no identifiable features—the nose, eyes, lips—nothing could be distinguished. It seemed like a patch of black smoke had gathered above her throat. He panicked. There was no one around. Looking back, he was shocked to see that the woman had vanished from where she was just a moment ago. He decided to go back the way he came. But as soon as he turned back, he saw the woman once again. She was walking toward him with her hands raised, as if she intended to kill him.

The primary attraction of the Hahim is that the place was built around the sole purpose of people coming over for a picnic, a short trip to cook, eat, enjoy, and roam around the sights. Potable water, combustion fuel for cooking, shade for relaxing—everything is very easily available in this place. But this group of people who came here to enjoy the day were thrown into a pit of anxiety and tension. A member of their group has gone missing. It was not especially crowded, and he was not the kind of guy who would leave without notifying a single person. His phone too, was out of network coverage.

Shantanu's brother could not keep track of how long he ran at a stretch, but when he gathered his senses together, he found himself in a sunny place, profusely panting and sweating. Did he just come back from a different time, a different place? Evening had coexisted with day, hypnotizing him into walking an endless path, pulling him deeper into a different realm! Who was that woman? It was not possible for any human being to appear like that.

He tried to remember the way he came from and walked back to rejoin the group he was supposed to be with now. He shared his experience with the curious, anxious crowd despite knowing that he could never possibly express exactly what he had experienced. When he was halfway through the story, one guy came forward and stretched his hand and demanded to share a little of what he was smoking. Feeling a bit embarrassed and insulted, he never spoke about the incident in front of his friends again.

Shantanu knew his brother never intoxicated himself with any kind of substances. He firmly believes that something really happened to this brother on that day in Hahim. He knows that even to this day, his brother keeps looking back to check if someone is following him while he walks on any road. And that is the reason why Shantanu did not want to pick Hahim as the destination for their group picnic this winter.

9

MALCHA MAHAL: A SAD, CURSED HISTORY

Delhi's Malcha Mahal was built in 1325 under Firoz Shah Tughlaq as a hunting lodge. Located in present-day Delhi's Chanakyapuri, this shikargah or hunting place got its name from Malcha, a historical village where it was built. Over the years, it has also been called Bistadari Mahal and Wilayat Mahal after the begum who took possession of it in 1985. Begum Wilayat Mahal claimed to be the great-granddaughter of the last nawab of Awadh, Wajid Ali Shah. When the British took over Awadh, the royal property was seized. Begam Wilayat Mahal lay claim to the ancestral properties of the Nawab's family and wanted the government to allot her Malcha Mahal as compensation. She came to Delhi to reclaim what the government owed her. She took shelter in the waiting lounge at the Delhi Railway Station and stayed there in protest for nine years. Finally, in May 1985 the Government of India granted her the ownership of Malcha Mahal. She moved in with her son, Ali and daughter, Sakina and quite a few pet dogs who guarded their new residence.

Malcha Mahal would have faded from public memory if not for the events that followed. In 1993, Begum Wilayat Mahal committed suicide, reportedly by consuming diamond dust. Her children, Sakina and Ali Raza, could not accept the passing of their mother. They took her body and placed her on the study table—perhaps they thought their mother would wake up or they were not in a state to comprehend the difference between life and death. It was only after about ten days that the news broke out in the neighbourhood and the locals arranged for the begum's burial. The suicide made Malcha Mahal a topic of gossip, The people became curious about what could have led to Begum Wilayat Mahal's decision and how she had survived in relative seclusion with only her children and pet dogs for company. Some miscreants even tried digging up her grave, expecting to find some treasure.

Ali and Sakina continued to live a private, secluded life in Malcha Mahal after their mother's death. Being surrounded by the Ridge forest, this palace was not connected to electricity or water supply. It is clear that the two passed their days in poverty. They didn't come in contact with other people; a sign outside the property warned 'intruders shall be gunned down'. Their fierce hounds roamed freely in the yard, scaring away thieves and any curious outsiders who may have thought of breaking in. Devoid of any human connections for several years, Sakina was the first to pass away. In 2017, police found the lonely dead body of Ali Raza, sitting on a sofa in the living room of the ruined palace. Though nobody figured out exactly when and how he passed away, the police reported that he had a normal death. There was no burial ceremony and the self-proclaimed last heir of the once-prosperous nawab of Awadh was laid to rest with the help of money from the Waqf Board. The decrepit Mahal carried minimal belongings: old furniture, piles of worn-out papers, a few utensils, and some photographs.

It is rumoured that a strange light flickers in the Mahal and sharp screams can be heard from inside. Despite their curiosity, people's fear and uneasiness about this ruin prevents them from venturing inside. A royal lineage, reclaimed inheritance, and the subsequent suicide and deaths—these are the landmarks in the cursed history of Malcha Mahal or Wilayat Mahal. Only time will tell whether people continue to believe the place is haunted.

10

TUNNEL NUMBER 33

Susmita was eager to visit the mountains after her wedding. She had been following several blogs about Himachal tourism. She had even made a list of hotels from the available apps and kept making trip-related suggestions to her husband, Partha. Susmita had wanted to go on a tour long before they got married, but with all the chores that needed to be completed before and after the wedding ceremony, it had been postponed repeatedly. They had been to some nearby places but those getaways barely lasted a day or two. She wanted an opportunity to test out her skills with the camera, so she was looking forward to visiting somewhere picturesque and out of the ordinary. It was Partha who had sparked her interest in photography, and gradually Susmita had overtaken him with her fascination with the different lenses and frames of the camera. Both of them were excited to capture the mountains, the glossy ice, the gorgeous greenery, and the daybreak from the hilltop. Susmita had read that the Tunnel Number 33 in Shimla was one of the most remarkable haunted places in India. Being a fan of horror stories from an early age, she became very eager to see this place with her own eyes.

After many nights of anticipation, the day finally came when the happy couple arrived in Shimla. They had planned a long tour that would cover as many spots in Himachal as possible. They visited the Ridge, the Himachal State Museum, and the Kali Bari Temple one by one and then it was time to visit Tunnel Number 33. They wanted to avoid going there when it was dark, so they fixed a time for the next afternoon. There are many stories concerning this tunnel on the Shimla–Kalka train route. The architectural excellence of this tunnel, built by the then British-Indian Government, is remarkable. Susmita had done some research about this place before they visited it. After all, she had high hopes from this haunted tunnel and couldn't just go with no expectations.

There are a total of a 102 tunnels throughout the train route between Shimla and Kalka. This track became operational in 1903. Years of planning of several engineers and the hard work of many workers contributed to the development of this marvel. Among these 102 tunnels, this is the longest one. Tunnel Number 33 is 1.14 kilometres long and its official name is Barog Tunnel. This name comes from Colonel Barog, who led the group of engineers and workers over a century ago when this tunnel was built. It is believed that the ghost of Colonel Barog, unable to let go of his affection towards the place, still roams here. Some people can still spot him around the tunnel.

In 1898, Barog, an engineer with the railway company, was given responsibility of building this tunnel. It was not an easy task to dig through the mountain and build a tunnel that would withstand the test of time and allow trains full of passengers to pass through for years. There were strict deadlines for finishing the job, and the surrounding mountain was never in favour of him. After many calculations, Barog determined the mining spots on two sides of the mountain and the work began to clear out a path for the tunnel. The work was progressing fairly fast, but as the deadline neared, it was discovered that the two ends that were being dug would never meet. There were some mistakes in his calculations and no alternative methods gave him any hope.

Failing to meet the deadline, Colonel Barog was held responsible for wasting time and government resources. The authority penalized him with a fine of one Indian rupee. Barog's professional pride was completely ruined and he thought very low of himself. This put him in a state of depression. One afternoon, when he went out to walk his dog, he ended his own life with a gun.

Colonel Barog was buried near the tunnel he was so passionate about building but had failed to complete. Later, a different team of engineers took up the responsibility and made fresh calculations to complete the tunnel. They moved one end of the tunnel and completed Barog's unfinished work. Barog's soul did not abandon his work. He remained at this place. He remained in the minds of the people who worked with him and those who believed in him. His soul still roams around his old workplace that caused him so much pain, depression, and eventually led to his death. People can still spot his shadow while passing through this tunnel. Some people even claim that the Englishman's spirit sometimes speaks to people. The government has tried to close down this tunnel several times, but strangely, it is always reopened after a short time. Being the longest tunnel, it requires frequent maintenance. It does not matter how many lights are put in the tunnel; it is never amply lit up. Even to this day, the workers arrange for light using mirrors and reflectors to navigate sunlight into this place to continue their work.

Susmita studied these stories keenly and shared them with Partha. Partha smirked and said, 'A strange place like this, the history from such a long time ago mingled with the story of a suicide and a nearby grave. It is very natural that this tunnel would be accompanied by some spooky stories.' He was not ready to believe any of the stories. His hypothesis suggested that even if someone actually saw something here, it would be under the influence of these stories and may be a figment of the imagination. The couple reached the Barog station in the afternoon. They went on a car and their plan was to take a train through this tunnel on their way back. There were a few people around and the station looked beautiful during sunset. Susmita took permission from the railway staff nearby to capture some photos of the station and the tunnel. She took many pictures of the station and the surrounding landscape with the sun setting behind the mountains.

The tunnel began at the far end of the platform. The train arrived in a while and Susmita and Partha got on. When they were going through the long, dark tunnel, the sound of the wheels echoed in rhythm. Susmita stuck out the lens of her camera through the window rails and took a few photos of the tunnel. Where was the ghost? There was nothing creepy about that beautiful, calm place. A cold breeze flowed as evening gently covered everything with the shawl of darkness.

Later, as the couple sat on their bed sharing a mug of hot chocolate, Partha advised Susmita to transfer the photos from her camera to the laptop so she would have space to take more photos in the following days. This gave them a chance to go through all the shots that she took.

Susmita was pleased with how the photos had turned out. She had captured the beautiful sky, and the sunset at the station and the sunlight falling on the face of the tunnel. She was staring at this photo when she noticed something that freaked her out. She pointed her finger at the screen. There was a white Englishman standing in front of the tunnel staring back at them. Susmita's finger struck the delete button in fear. Did Partha see him too?

11

THE SCREAM IN AVADH PALACE

Horror stories often spread through word of mouth. Many such stories are set in places of historical significance and are responsible for creating a myth around those sites. There are several tourist attractions that are considered haunted, and although some people may avoid them out of fear, the stories add to their popularity. One such place is the Avadh Palace located in the city of Rajkot in Gujarat.

The stories about Avadh Palace are so well known in the region that even in the absence of any proof or witness to supernatural activity, fear of this palace runs deep in people's minds. Some tourists who know the stories about this place make it a point to visit, others specifically avoid it for the same reason. This long-abandoned palace was once built for the purpose of hosting the guests of an aristocratic family but it was shut down for some mysterious reasons sometime after that. It is rumoured that the owners of this palace are NRIs. Fear about this palace is well-established among people. Like other haunted places, Avadh Palace also has an incident in its past and that has left a lasting negative impression among people.

Many years ago, a woman was tortured and brutally murdered inside this palace. Since then, her shadow can be seen around the palace. Ghosts returning to remind others of their lives or to exact vengeance is a common theme in many horror stories. With the oppression and violence faced by women in society, we come across many ghost stories about women. In this case, the cruelty of the crime is perceptible through the painful cries and wails that echo through the palace. The incident was so brutal that it is bound to make one fear fellow humans. Many people refuse to set foot on the grounds of Avadh Palace; they are afraid of witnessing something supernatural. There aren't many with a first-hand experience to share but there are countless stories about the palace. People say that a strange woman is seen walking around in the palace after dark. Sometimes, a sharp, painful scream can be heard from the palace.

Another story goes like this. One curious young student was eager to explore this building to verify the veracity of the rumours about the ghost. He walked inside the front door of the boundary one evening and began looking around. He saw a young woman inside. He thought that the ghost stories could be a front for suspicious activities and decided to follow the woman. She was slowly walking towards the main building. As soon as they reached the entrance to the main building, the woman vanished. He looked around but could not find a trace of her. He continued to walk but just as he was about to set foot near the door, his ears rang from the loud shriek of a woman. It was a cry for help. It sounded as if she was still fighting for her life with all her might. The doors and windows were vibrating from the intensity of that sound. Gradually, the shriek died down, indicating the obvious. After this experience, the boy did not wait a moment longer. He turned around and ran out of there.

Whether the ghost actually exists is not as relevant a question as how such a heinous crime could take place. We would stop hearing new horror stories like this when crimes against women are stopped, when no ghosts are compelled to relive their torment and confront society for the ills committed against them.

12

PARI TIBBA: A TALE OF UNFULFILLED LOVE

Pari Tibba is a famous hill east of Mussoorie, close to the cantonment town of Landour. The word 'Pari' means fairy and the place is also known as Hill of the Fairies. It is a picturesque hill covered with oaks and deodars and breathtaking views that finds mention in many stories by Ruskin Bond. Visiting this place is easy if you're looking for a destination for trekking. One can reach Pari Tibba by taking the road beside Woodstock school, close to Dhanaulti hill station. A small village called Dhobi Gaon falls on the way. Most residents of this village are dhobis, washermen, employed at the hotels and resorts in Mussoorie, Dhanualti, and other tourist spots. Walking through this village, one is likely to see houses decorated with clothings of various types and colours hung from the edges of the roofs, in verandas, and the yards for drying. A forest route from this village leads to Pari Tibba. The narrow, winding forest route is so calm and silent that sometimes even the falling of dry leaves is audible. Peeking through the clouds and the gaps between the trees, sunlight dapples the path. Tiny wildflowers blooming throughout the path make the walk pleasant. There are also many ruins of old houses along the path. Hills are more prone to lightning than other places; these stone-built houses lie in ruins because of storms. One of these houses witnessed an incident that was responsible for enlisting the beautiful Pari Tibba along with the places that instil fear in people.

Among the plethora of stories set around this hilltop, the most famous one is a love story with a sad conclusion. The abandoned roads near Pari Tibba indicate that the place used to be populated once upon a time and people would use these roads for their daily needs. A couple that had travelled to the hill took shelter in one of the abandoned houses. No one knows whether they were running away from somewhere or whether they just wanted a place to spend some time together undisturbed by anyone. A heavy storm hit that night and lightning struck the house, causing a fatal accident. People travelling on this road later discovered the burnt bodies of the couple from the abandoned house where they had taken shelter. This couple continues to let others know about their existence even after their bodies met with an unfortunate death. Their story can be heard from the turns of the winding mountain route and the plants across the forest.

At any place with a history like this, stories spread like wildfire among people. As this story was exchanged between people, newer stories kept being added to it over time. Among this group of stories, there is one that strikes a different chord. Unlike the others, this leaves listeners with a smile.

One evening, a couple got stuck in this place due to a heavy storm. They were trying to get down the hill, but with every passing moment the risk of danger increased with the sound of thunder and frequent lightning strikes. The surroundings began getting darker as the day neared evening. The couple were at a loss about how to descend from the hills. The road was a known winding route but the problem was how exactly they would proceed in these bad weather conditions. Suddenly, they saw two straight parallel lines on the ground in front of them. It looked like someone was dragging a stick through the soft mud. As they followed the direction of these lines, they saw another pair of lines appear. They began following those lines out of curiosity and as they kept stepping forward, more such lines kept appearing on the ground. The sky was pouring and the cold wind was roaring all over. There was lightning every other moment and intense thunder could be heard. Following those lines, they understood that they were being guided on the right track to descend from the hill. After walking some more time, they reached a safe place. The parallel lines showed them the way to safety. Who drew those lines and how could they do it? They did not see any person around but they strongly believed that the spirit of the couple who had lost their lives on the hill came to help them escape and save themselves. Their unfulfilled love never reached a happy ending, so they helped another couple find their way to safety.

Mussoorie, the queen of hills, is full of stories of light and darkness. With the passing of time, new incidents and tales are added to them when people share them over a cup of tea. The heavenly Pari Tibba is an excellent destination for a weekend trek and also a centre for mildly haunted tales. The unfortunate couple is just one of the many ghosts you may encounter here.

13

THE TEARS AT NOHKALIKAI FALLS

Some incidents leave such great impacts that they remain a topic of discussion for ages to come. Even if it did not happen right in front of our eyes, its existence in history ensures that it is carried forward by people. An ordinary spot's history can uncover a long forgotten past and make it stand out in the neighbourhood. There are many stories like this spread across India. Some of these stories come from folklore, and some of them have secured their place in history. Such a deadly but beautiful story flows underneath the Nohkalikai falls, located in the state of Meghalaya.

Nohkalikai falls is the highest waterfall in India and it is also among the tallest waterfalls across the globe. Situated at a distance of about seven and half kilometres from Cherrapunji town, at an elevation of 1,239 metres above sea level, the waterfall has a drop of about 340 metres and the stream is almost 23 metres wide. The water flows into a green coloured lake. The place is an astounding beauty of nature. The waterfall and the associated stream are fed by the rainfall and so, the fall is at its best during monsoon. Although Cherrapunji has no shortage of rain at any time of the year, yet, the best five months for this place would be from May to September. The beautiful eye-soothing lake has a sad history attached to it. In Khasi, the words 'Noh ka Likai' translate to 'the leap of Likai'. Likai's sacrifice by jumping into this waterfall was the reason for its name.

The story dates back centuries ago. A girl named Likai lived in a village called Rangjyrteh. The village was located close to this waterfall. Probably the girl played a little in the water, maybe some days she just enjoyed the beauty of it and wondered where all the water flowed to, on her way across the stream. Likai was widowed at a very young age. She had a little daughter. The sudden burden of bearing the cost of living for herself as well as her family fell on her. She prepared herself to make a living in order to survive the world. Being busy with work most of the time, she could not pay enough attention to her infant. Some of her well-wishers told her that with the double burden of raising an infant and providing for the family, she was unable to fulfil either with the required proficiency. They advised her remarry to start it all over. After giving it a thought, Likai decided to get married once again, so that she could take better care of her child. But the plan backfired completely. Her awful husband cost her the life of her child as well as her own. The locals still believe that it is Likai's tears that flow with the water of this fall. Many people think, despite there being no proof, that a mad woman wanders around this waterfall. With tears in her eyes, she whispers in search of her infant child. People see her for a moment or two and then she vanishes either behind the waterfall or into the flowing water. A human cannot disappear that fast without jumping into the stream. She keeps returning to this place, as if by sacrificing her own life, she tried to condemn her failure to protect her baby.

Her decision to get remarried in order to take care of her daughter was the very reason for her undoing. One day, after returning home from work, Likai's husband told her that he had cooked a special meal just for her. Her husband's thoughtful gesture made her wonder where her baby had gone. Maybe she had gone to the neighbours to play with her friends. Likai thought that after she had finished the meal, she would go out to bring her child back home. After the meal, Likai went to prepare the betel leaf as she did every day. Going near her ingredients, she received a shock. A little finger of a child was there in the basket, among the betel nuts. Likai instantly understood what had happened. Her husband had killed the baby and then minced her body, cooked it, and fed it to Likai. Likai lost her sanity when she realized what her new husband had done. She hit her own head repeatedly with a hammer she found in the house. She ran out beside the stream. Being unable to bear the immeasurable pain and grief of what she was made to do, Likai jumped into the stream near the waterfall.

All her hopes and dreams for a better life for her child, as well as her grief, drowned in the water with her. After this sad, gory, and inhumane incident, this waterfall was named Nohkalikai to remember this helpless mother.

The waterfall is a symbol of a mother's sorrow. Standing here, it is baffling to think that even in this place of such mesmerizing beauty and bliss, immeasurable human cruelty exists. Being jealous of a child from the wife's first marriage, killing her, and feeding the cooked flesh of a child to her own mother! How cruel can a human being be? There is nothing to prove that the spirit of Likai roams around the waterfall but the tale has been immortalized by the name it bears.

14

THAT SHADOW IN THE MATERNITY WARD

'Have you finished your round?'

'Yes. I completed one round in this ward just now. I'll take another walk a little late in the night. The day has been so tiring...I want to take a nap in this room.'

Akash took a look around the room and then focused on the bed. So much had changed over time, but nobody had bothered to change the yellow lamp in there. It was a relief that somebody changed the bedsheet. He was carrying a bottle of water with him. After disconnecting the call, he walked over and sat on the bed. He was rarely allotted shifts at night and even if he was, the work mostly comprised of taking a couple of walks around the ward and the rest of the time passed in this cabin. He had come to this room before, but that was mostly to pass the time gossiping with some colleagues. This was the first time he came here to sleep. The patients were all asleep in the emergency ward, the nurses were on duty. Taking a nap now would help him keep his body fully functional throughout the shift. The yellow lamp was so dim that it wouldn't hinder his slumber. Akash put his phone off silent mode and put it on the table. As soon as he laid his body on the bed and closed his eyes, he fell asleep.

There was a long corridor right outside the door which was not well-lit. There was a balcony to the left of the corridor that looked on to the lonely street outside the hospital. A turn at the balcony led to the emergency room, and the maternity ward was further down. Akash had checked all of these sections while completing his round of the floor.

The time was around half past one. Akash's woke up suddenly. He felt that someone had called him. Who would call him up from this room? Did the phone just ring? Before he could figure out anything, he sensed as if someone was talking to him a moment ago and walked out of the door. Was it something important? He hurriedly walked out of the room and walked to the emergency ward. Akash asked a nurse if someone from there had called him. The nurse was surprised, she was dozing off, and nobody had gone to his room. She seemed a little scared. There were rumours that some people had been experiencing strange things in this hospital for months. And this is the very ward where....

The incident happened during the monsoon. A patient in the maternity ward was scheduled for her delivery the next day, but the nurses were informed to remain alert as the patient was facing some complications. It was raining heavily and the wind was roaring. A few minutes past one o'clock, the woman started experiencing agonizing pain. The doctors and nurses were able to save the mother, but the baby could not survive. The mother broke down completely. Anybody who looked at that face could feel the immense pain she felt. The woman stopped talking to anyone after that and almost stopped eating any of her food. She was recovering as days passed by when the incident happened. She jumped off the balcony and ended all of her pain altogether.

Everyone who was admitted to this ward felt a little uneasy. Some of them heard her crying in the middle of the night, others sensed her presence but couldn't see her. But there were others who did not face anything strange.

Akash went to the maternity ward. Who had called him? The matter did not need much explanation. The sister in-charge had warned him not to go into that room alone at night. Akash had spent years studying skeletons and dead-bodies and now after all this, he was scared of ghosts? Of all things? He had heard about the suicide…he had looked after that patient for a few days. Akash asked the nurse if she had heard about such experiences from anybody else. She waited a couple of moments before she spoke up. One of her colleagues had spotted the shadow of a woman walking through the aisle but found nobody when she followed the shadow. A few days back, one of the janitors looked up from the street and saw a woman looking down from the balcony, but she vanished a moment later. And just that day, she herself had heard the crying of a woman when she was in the washroom, she followed the sound and ended up near the balcony but there was no one around.

After some time Akash's eyelids were feeling heavy once again. He felt a little angry at himself. As a doctor, he should not be allowing these kinds of superstitions and false beliefs. Even if there was something happening, he should be the one investigating and finding out the reason behind the phenomenon. He walked past the balcony. There were a few people walking around the street, and the glowing signs were visible from everywhere. Akash returned to the room with the dim yellow light. The light has gotten so faint over time that he was barely able to distinguish anything inside. He partially closed the door and rested on the bed. He thought he would sleep the instant he closed his eyes, but that did not happen. He tossed and turned a couple of times, yawning repeatedly. Just when he was about to fall asleep, he heard someone whispering, someone speaking very softly very close to him. Startled, he sat up in an instant. He looked around. There was nobody. He thought he was hallucinating. He saw a shadow on the wall. He assumed it was his shadow from the yellow light as he was sitting upright on the bed. He yawned again and laid his body on the bed. The sleepiness was gone, he understood that he would not be able to sleep anymore for now. He thought of getting up and spending the rest of the night in the ward and chatting away with the other staff. But when he turned to face the wall, he spotted the shadow still standing there. Whose shadow was that? He focused on it to discern the shape of a woman and he began hearing the whisper again. This time he listened carefully, it is a feeble woman pleading, 'Doctor, please save my baby! My only baby! Please doctor....'

Akash's limbs started to tremble. Taking the phone in his hand, he was ready to jump out of the bed, just then, the shadow moved from the wall. Now it was on the door and the very next moment it vanished. Akash started breathing heavily in a mix of fear and helplessness. He rushed to the half-closed door and slammed it open. The shadow was waiting for him in the balcony and the whispering continued, 'doctor, please...please save my baby....' When he approached the balcony, the shadow began walking around, it took a shape, released from the bounds of any wall or surface. Before his boggled mind could comprehend anything, the shadow seemed to turn around and look him once in the eyes and the next instant, it climbed on the railing and jumped. Akash was frozen.

Some time had passed in that shocked state. Akash managed to gather his wits and courage somehow. He rushed to the ward but barely managed to express what he had seen and heard. All that he did was to keep himself from fainting by telling himself that what he experienced could not be conveyed to anybody else. After a few days, Akash submitted a written application to fix the lighting in that room and the aisle. After that day, whenever he had night shifts, he would sleep as much as he could during the day so that he wouldn't need to go to that room at night. Still, sometimes when he comes out to that balcony, he is startled by a whisper, 'doctor, please save my baby....'

15

THE WITCH IN JAGATPURA

Jaipur is known as the Pink City. This city which was built by and for the royal families is the capital of the state of Rajasthan. Established in 1727, Jaipur attracts tourists from all over the nation. This capital has its own share of historical elements. Many incidents have taken place in the city as time has passed. And naturally, a good number of them have a supernatural element. A place called Jagatpura demands special attention. This business centre has some really mysterious tales. People have spotted a strange person walking along on the streets at night. When the night gets thicker, people become afraid of going out at all, they suddenly spot a white-clothed woman beside them. She creeps on the road with very small steps while her messy hair float in the breeze. And if someone looks closely, they would see that her feet face backwards. Even if she takes steps forward with time, her destination seems to remain in the past. The story of this witch is attached to the name of the place where she keeps appearing, Jagatpura. And the tale is so widespread that people who visit Jaipur often take out some time from their trip to have a look at this place.

Prejudice and superstition have caused the deaths of many innocent people suspected of witchcraft throughout the world. That is why, in today's world, instead of believing in the existence of witches and wizards, we should be finding the causes behind these beliefs. There could be any number of reasons for the longevity of such beliefs among the people residing here. It all starts with an incident that induces fear. Similarly, in Jagatpura, we find an old story which is behind the fear. Even people who have never seen anything strange themselves, but have heard of others' experiences, count Jagatpura as a haunted place. All residents may not have any first-hand experiences to share, but there are multiple stories surrounding this place, spanning multiple decades.

Once this place had a tyrannical, greedy ruler. The subjects spent their lives in grave misery and poverty under him. Many people were forced to starve by the tyrant ruler. A popular belief claims that the souls of these helpless people who had to meet a painful, untimely death because of the carelessness and torment of their ruler have returned to make their presence felt in Jagatpura. As time passed, the representation of those wandering souls has converted into a figure of a witch. The mysterious walking woman is counted as a witch only because of her appearance, and not due to other activities associated with witches in mainstream tales.

Quite a few stories are circulated in this area about the strange experiences of some people. One guy encountered a supernatural entity on his way home at night and his story came to be accepted as truth. He was a bit scared by the sight of a lonely woman walking on the road at night, draped in a tall, white dress. She was walking very slowly. As a decent man, to avoid being suspected as a follower, he turned up his pace of walking to overtake the woman on the road. But he realized, no matter how fast he walked, he could not overtake the woman in the white dress. He felt that there was something unusual about her. Her messy hair was floating in the air. She seemed to be walking very slowly, but he could, in no way, overtake her. Wondering what was wrong, he suddenly noticed that the woman's feet were facing backwards. The guy could not believe his own eyes. Her heels were facing the way she was walking but her toes were facing the opposite direction. He could not gather the courage to take another step, he ran in the opposite direction and rang the bell at a random neighbour's house to get a temporary shelter. After this incident, more people have reported witnessing a woman walking on the street at night, wearing long white clothes. Since then, people do not dare going out after the sun sets. Even if they absolutely need to get out, they find someone to accompany them.

If you try to discuss these stories during your visit to Jagatpura, people may laugh it off, saying that having a woman in white walking alone at night like Bollywood horror movies would be way too dramatic to be anything close to reality. But the fear of spotting such a figure is prominent among the people who have lived here for a long time, regardless of the truthfulness of the stories. Nobody knows why this witch keeps returning to the place. The stories transcend time to become popular beliefs. This 'popular belief' is responsible for making a place haunted.

16

THREE KINGS CHAPEL

Goa is the heart of the Indian tourism industry. Lots of foreign tourists visit year-round. The beaches are always charged up and energetic with lots of tourists from India and abroad. This place still bears the signs of the Portuguese who ruled over here for a long time. From the buildings to the livelihood of the people, the effects are noticeable.

Hundreds of stories prevail alongside the old mansions, churches along the turns of the roads, the hotels near the beaches, and the highways. The lonely man with an old scooter still sighs gazing at his long shadow under the street lamp, away from the lively nightlife of Goa. Tales of the past are told and retold for generations. Some stories hold their eeriness to this time. The houses built in between the greenery are painted with their own legends. Apart from the tourist attractions, the Baytakhol and Rodrigues houses are notable. The Three Kings Chapel demands a special mention. This Three Kings Chapel has not only its beauty but also a story of darkness and horror associated with it.

This Chapel, surrounded by tales from three kings, would put anybody in awe. A long, winding road leads to this place. Everywhere you look, there is greenery spread around with the sea roaring in the background. The afternoon sun turns red and merges with the sea at the horizon. A lot of modern tourists do not know about the horror stories surrounding this church, but the locals and those who are a little curious about the history never mark this place as just a tourist site.

Cansaulim is a village located in the southern part of Goa. And along the coast of Cansaulim runs the hill named Cuelim. The bright white chapel, located on the hill in this calm place, can be spotted from the road. A scooter can be your best travel partner when wandering around Goa. Once you take the turn and start going uphill, the weather cools down fast. After travelling further, you can spot some eagles flying around in the sky and a few tourists here and there. Nobody wants to stay in this place after sunset, regardless of their beliefs in the existence of the supernatural. The view from the front of the Chapel is heavenly. One way it's all hills clustered together and the other way you see the city. One moment your attention would swim to the fishing boats in the sea, and suddenly it would hop among the happy trees waving their leaves under the evening breeze. There is a green field after crossing a gate, and further down the field is a small town. These people carry the stories of why nobody visits the chapel after evening, the stories of the strange sounds that keep coming from the place at night, and the cursed history of the place.

It was a time when Goa was a Portuguese colony. Naturally, the rulers had a significant influence on the culture and lifestyle of everyone in the territory. The incident with the three kings took place during that regime. The primary motive of all three kings was to win the throne. While the region was still in unrest, King Holger Alvunger invited the other two majesties for a discussion over dinner. The other two kings saw the hope of a peaceful understanding and arrived for the meeting. But Alvunger's true goal was to get rid of his competition. He planned the event and poisoned the food intended for those two kings. Once he cleared his hurdles, he declared himself king over the entire territory of the three kingdoms.

The misdeed did not remain buried for long. People were not ready to accept a merciless, cowardly usurper who killed the other kings in an unfair way as their king. The murderous crowd chased him out of the throne and drove him into the confinement of this chapel. Having no servant by his side and nothing else to eat and drink, he accidentally ate the poisoned drinks and food that were left over from the time he put the other kings to death. He met his end at his own hands.

All three of the fighting kings heard their death bell ring in this chapel. The subjects of the kingdom buried all of them in the graveyard here. And since that time this chapel has been known as the 'Three Kings Chapel'. A few people come to this chapel for worship and they have shared their experiences about hearing some voices speaking in a strange language from the other side of the door. The stories have been alive and circulating for decades. The locals believe that the souls of the three dead kings roam around this place to this day and that is why nobody stays here after dusk.

Maybe there is nothing to be afraid of, maybe it is just a hoax that received validation from long-standing public beliefs. There is no proof whether anybody ever saw anything within the confines of this chapel. The places with supernatural entities live on in stories like this, the eeriness of such places can be felt when the cold evening breeze chills a wary traveller. It surely does give one an uneasy feeling to look around the vast hills when taking a walk on the road to the chapel. This lonely chapel on a barren hilltop will surely keep its place in your memory if you step near these roads.

17

MAYONG VILLAGE

The practice of black magic is still alive in Mayong village in Assam. Despite the development of science and technology, Mayong is a strange place that stands out with ancient dark practices. This is a village located by the banks of Brahmaputra River, in the Morigaon district in Assam. This place, forty kilometres from Guwahati, has been mentioned several times in the Puranas. The village was famous among a lot of travellers because of the mysteries it held, which the Puranas mention, and also because of the wildlife that made it their home. The Pobitora Wildlife Sanctuary of Assam is home to the one-horned rhinoceros or great Indian rhinoceros. In 2002, the Mayong Central Museum and Emporium of Black Magic and Witchcraft was established to uphold the traditions of this village. One can find weapons, old coins, tools used for rituals and human sacrifice, jewellery made from human skulls and bones that the dark magic practitioners used to wear during performing the rituals, and a lot more in this museum.

The name Mayong is said to have originated from the Sanskrit word 'maya', which means illusion. In some of the local languages, the word 'Mayong' means the mother-goddess and some etymologists believe that the name originated from this word instead. Apart from these two beliefs, there is another theory. Groups of people who travelled from Manipur and became residents of this place were locally known as Mairang and there is a good possibility that this place got its name from a derivation of the word.

But what's in a name? Illusions, secrets, and mysteries have occupied Mayong for a long time. In the fourteenth century, Muhammad Shah attacked the state of Assam with his army of numerous horse riders. Mysteriously, the entire army vanished into thin air when they reached Mayong. The tradition of human sacrifice for religious rituals has been alive here for ages. There are stories of vanishing humans, and people being converted into some kind of animals and then let out to roam around the place as strays. The traditions of black magic, astrology, and mantra-tantra have been passed down generations like family traditions here.

The ojhas and gunin, divine medicine men, are believed to have the powers to cure many critical illnesses. Despite curing diseases, they don't call themselves doctors but prefer to go by the name of ojha and gunin. Their process of healing is also strange. Looking from the outside, it seems like a combination of some plants and roots in brassware.

A young lad visited Mayong with his group of friends in the hope of capturing some great photographs for his freelance career. This is a story that came from his experience.

For treating patients, these ojhas tie up a brass bowl on the ailing part of the patient's body. If there is pain and agony, this treatment is further enforced in such cases. The ojhas or the kabiraj would chant some mantras and proceed to ask the bowl to eat up the pain. There are some treatments where the medic would keep a ghost or a supernatural spirit as their assistant. In these cases, the ghost is like one of their pets. One such case was when a man was so agonized by joint pain that he was almost immobilized. The guy could not even stand up. One of these Kabiraj did the brassware procedure to heal him. A few days later, the man was able to stand up and walk once again.

Another reason people come to this place is to look for clues to find some valuable things that they have lost. When someone loses something precious to them, they ask the ojhas to help them find it. The ojha then puts a flower in a metallic container and asks it to find the lost item after enchanting it with some mantras. Right after receiving the order, the metallic container slowly starts rolling towards the lost item and provides a direction to look in to find it.

Coming from the big cities, this photographer and his friends curiously watched these practices but they could believe in none of them. A constant doubt worked within one of them. His opinion was, either the entire process is fake or this was a scam to fool people. The man was nearly determined to expose the fraud that was going on. He put the lens of his camera in the bag and went to an aged ojha. The ojha sat in a small hut, the interior of the room was pretty dim even during the day. A tiny oil lamp was trying hard to illuminate the space from a far corner of the room. The ojha and his wife had been in this profession for a good amount of time. The photographer lamented about losing the precious and expensive lens of his camera and requested the ojha to help him find it. The lens was, in reality, inside his bag. The old man asked where he saw the lens for the last time. The man said he went into the woods to take some photographs and changed the lens there, since then, he has been unable to find the old lens that he detached. The old man put a flower in the brass bowl placed in front of him and closed his eyes. The wife brought the oil lamp from the corner of the room to his front. He started chanting shlokas and waving his hand. The shadow on the wall was moving with the unsteady flame of the lamp and the waving of the arm. The bowl made a startling sound. The old man spoke with his eyes closed, 'The thing you have lost can be seen under a very dim light that is escaping through the foliage, between two trees, inside the jungle'. The man who came to test the ojha looked at his friend and let out a smirk. When the bowl spun up and went out through the door, the old man stood. The guy laughed aloud and said, 'I don't need to go anywhere, I have my lens with me, right here, in this bag'. The old man paused for a moment and stopped chanting mantras. He turned around in slow steps and looked at the guy who asked him to find it. His eyes had a strange stare. There were no signs of anger, disappointment, or disturbance. It was just an empty, vacant stare. The old man refused to take any money for performing this ritual, he gently took the flower from the bowl and kept it aside. When coming out of the hut, the photographer felt a little sorry for the old man, he seemed helpless. The entire thing could be a scam but disrespecting an old man after coming into his house did not seem like a very wise thing to do.

A couple of days later, the day came for them to return. The train was scheduled to depart at night, and they would reach home by morning. They had captured a lot of photos and collected a good amount of material to further study and write articles. After boarding the train, they located their berths and then proceeded to count all their belongings one final time before leaving the state.

They could find their cameras and all the equipment, except that one lens the man hid in his bag to trick the old ojha. In its place there was a hard and unusually shaped item. The man took out everything he had in the bag and started to count the items. Only one lens was missing and, in its place, there was a familiar looking brass bowl with bits of dirt on it.

This village of Mayong, that is filled with maya, illusion, is a place that still practices tantra-mantra, occultism, and dark magic. A unique strand of Indian culture is still alive and being continued in this place, and that is more important than finding whether it is true or a scam.

18

KASARA GHAT

Kasara ghat is located near Kasara and Igatpuri towns. These two towns are connected by a highway and Kasara Ghat can be reached from it. This is the same highway that connects Mumbai and Nasik as well. From Nasik to Mumbai, it is the shortest spanning route a traveller can take among the three ways available. Within this one 167-kilometres highway, this 14-kilometre-long portion has a strange, eerie vibe lurking around it after the sun sets. The usage of the road has never stopped, but a lot of people avoid travelling through this route during the night. Maybe there is something lingering in the air? Many accidents along this route are responsible for listing it among haunted places. Is there really something on this road? Is there really something worth mentioning about Kasara Ghat again and again?

There are several valid reasons behind the high number

of accidents on this road. The asphalt gets damaged due to heavy rainfall around these places. Potholes are formed on the road, making it even more dangerous. Due to the lack of law enforcement, lots of bikers do not follow the speed limit when travelling through here and that causes a lot of accidents. Just in the first half of the year 2021, over twenty people have been engulfed by death caused by road accidents that happened on this route. According to the police, the accidents were caused by breaking road rules, driving on the wrong side of the road, parking the vehicles at random places, along with the bad condition of the road. The monsoons are harsh in the Western Ghats and no matter how many times the road is repaired, it deteriorates soon enough. Despite these explanations, we can never be sure whether those people had seen or experienced anything supernatural before the accidents took place. Could something have suddenly appeared right before the vehicles in the dead of the night causing those accidents?

Numerous people travel on this road and come out alive, having experienced nothing strange. The mystery surrounding this place originates from the reccurring accidents and deaths and the rumour that criminals used to dispose of dead bodies by the sides of this road a long time ago. All these stories and rumours have lent a strange atmosphere of fear to this place. Even if someone claims to have seen some supernatural entity around this place, there would be no proof of it. Year after year, new stories begin circulating, new posts come live on social media, and most of them bear the same tone.

During the night, especially on amavasya, the day before the new moon, the lurking spirits of people who lost their lives to unfortunate events like road accidents, become powerful. They begin influencing the passers-by. It is assumed that the spirits lost some of their body parts in the accidents that killed them. The shadows that suddenly disappear under the bright headlamp right after taking a turn during a night journey frighten the rider.

Sometimes people notice something moving on top of the large trees and pause on their way while crossing the road at night. They get down from the vehicle and try to figure out what they just saw and after a few seconds of staring, they shiver in realization that what they are seeing is a woman sitting on a branch, with her long legs dangling. A daring person once approached the tree to get a better look, and possibly dismiss the fear, but what he made out was a feeble, old woman. Most people try to leave the place as fast as they can. An exploration reveals something deadlier. It is really an old woman, sitting on a tree branch with her legs dangling from two sides of the branch, but the woman is missing a neck and a head. It is a headless body. There could be something more to this story, but the ones who took another step towards the woman are not in a position to share their experience. None of them made it back alive. After knowing this story, all the people who have sensed a similar occurrence dismiss their curiosity and get out of there as soon as they can.

Many people have written blogs and social media posts

about this highway stretching from Nasik to Mumbai. This place is among some of the popular haunted places of India. Explorers with a thirst for the supernatural take this route at night to possibly see something that they would not find anywhere else. One prominent difference that makes this place stand out from other haunted places is that a lot of accidents actually happen around here. It does not matter whether something eerie is present here or it's all just a hoax, a real fear clouds the minds of travellers who choose this route at night. There is no harm in being a bit more cautious while driving at night. Maybe this very alertness would save a person from a deadly accident. Maybe it would help them make it out alive.

19

THE HOUSE WORTH A HUNDRED AND FIFTY-THOUSAND

When one person is scared of a place there are a lot of counterarguments that could invalidate that fear. But what happens when the masses face the same fear and panic? Repeatedly? For a long time? No matter how many counterarguments in that case, the panic weighs down on them and the place is labelled haunted. This story is about a house with a turbulent history. The house is worth a hundred and fifty thousand. The name of the house is also its price, just a hundred and fifty thousand rupees. In today's market, imagining a house at this price is nearly impossible. The story of this house is about five decades old. A house is not just a structure, it comprises dreams and hopes, wishes that come true and a lot that don't. It includes hopes and ambitions crushed by harsh reality, but what happens if some fragment of a nightmare keeps coming back to haunt the people?

This eerie house worth a hundred and fifty thousand bucks is located in Hyderabad, not far from Secunderabad, at Seethaphalmandi. Almost all locals would recognize this house by its name in one go. Some would even ask you to not be too curious about this place. Strange sounds are often heard from this house, not just at night, but also during broad daylight.

Laxman was among the wealthy people in the locality. He decided to construct a spacious new building to live more comfortably with his wife and kids. All of them were involved in the thorough planning of the house. It cost them a hundred and fifty thousand rupees, which meant a lot back then. The house came to be named after its cost. It was a beautiful construction that was well recognized; some people even visited the place just to look at the house.

Once the construction was finished, Laxman and his family began preparing for the housewarming ceremony. But a mishap took place just before that ceremony. Even before setting her foot in the house which she had poured her heart into, Laxman's wife passed away due to a heart attack. Laxman's dream of living in his new house with his happy family shattered into pieces. He started to believe in the existence of an evil spirit in the building. He was convinced that this spirit was responsible for casting the shadow of bad luck over his family. He lost enthusiasm for the new house and decided not to move to the property. Instead, he rented it to a student for a low rent. In some time, people started noticing something strange about the behaviour of the young student living on that property. He had started walking differently, stopped talking to anyone, and always held a blank, vague stare. He was also losing weight at a concerning rate. He spoke to nobody, so no one knew what he was up to. Within a few days, people found out that the guy had committed suicide in the house.

People are scared to walk in front of that house after sunset. There is something strange and eerie about that place. Those who pass by the house recall seeing something horrible and are scared to return. Many years have passed but not a single person could happily live there. All tenants who came to stay there after that student either committed suicide or had an unnatural death.

There is one particular incident that scared people the most. One day, a man was walking in front of the house when the streetlights suddenly went dark. There was not a single person to be seen and the dogs were barking frantically. The man heard the sound of a door opening. He looked towards the house to find a woman standing in the balcony. Her loose hair was blowing in the wind and she had a fierce, cold stare. The man stood frozen for a moment. As the woman turned her gaze to him, he understood that this was no human being and ran for his life.

To this day, people from this locality do not step anywhere close to the house after dark. Rumours say that even the air feels different around there. The evil spirit in this house did not let a single person live there in peace.

The house worth a hundred and fifty thousand is above all the story of an unfulfilled dream. Laxman and his family's dream was shattered by fear of the unknown, and the people who tried to live in that house afterwards suffered the same fate. If you visit this place someday, you too may feel an uneasy breeze around this house. That sudden gust of wind may not carry a spirit, but it surely would carry a little bit of fear, and a scrape of sadness.

20

THAT OLD WOMAN FROM HOSKOTE ROAD

Hoskote used to be a jagir of Shahaji Raje, a Maratha warrior. Earlier known as Ooscota and Ooscata, it is located in the Rural Bangalore district of Karnataka. The first battle between the British and the kingdom of Mysore took place here in 1768. The Battle of Oosçota, as it was called, was fought between the British East India Company and the Mysore emperor Sultan Haider Ali. Apart from its historical significance, Hoskote is also famous for its ghost stories. There is one tree-lined road in particular where many frightening incidents have taken place. It is a scenic mountain road where the sun shines through the gaps between the dense trees. Bikers love this road but everyone who has had a supernatural experience believes that an unearthly being haunts this road. A local businessman used to frequently travel on the road, but he never imagined that he would witness something as inexplicable. While driving on the empty road one day, he spotted an old woman in the distance, she was slowly walking to the middle of the road. He blew the horn a few times but the old woman took no notice of it. He decided to slow down his bike and go around her. As he attempted to do so, the woman suddenly moved in front of his bike. Despite stopping the bike and blowing the loud horn, the woman did not budge. Irritated, the businessman started cursing her. The woman turned to face him and he could not believe what he saw next. The woman's body remained stationary while her head turned a hundred and eighty degrees. She stared at him with burning eyes. Within a moment, the businessman let go of his bike and started running away on foot. He could never make anyone believe what he had witnessed that day.

The existence of a graveyard beside the road fuels claims of supernatural activities. Many people's experiences on this road cannot be explained by logic or science. One such story has become so popular that it has practically turned into folklore. The story, narrated by an auto-rickshaw driver, is the one you'd undeniably come across on your journey to Hoskote.

The auto-rickshaw driver was returning home through the empty road after a long day. The sunlight was slowly dimming as dusk transitioned into a fine evening. Very few vehicles passed him by. The sky was beginning to get cloudy and the air felt misty. The driver had pasted photos of various deities on the windshield. A priest put some flowers there every morning before business began for the day. The driver was not in the mood to drive for much longer, he planned to roam about for twenty more minutes and then pick up a few passengers from the bus stop on his way home. He did not expect to find any passengers at this time on this road. A song was playing on the stereo but the driver did not feel like listening to it. He turned the stereo off. Once the music stopped, the calmness of the environment could be felt even more clearly. The humming of the auto's engine was the only disturbance in the silence. The auto's headlights were not too bright, the road was visible just for a short distance. After a few minutes, he felt like there was someone standing by the road. Driving ahead forward, he saw a woman waving her hand towards his auto. He stopped upon reaching her. The woman was pretty old, there was a shopping bag in her hand, and her hair was grey and dishevelled by the wind. Seeing the auto coming to a stop, she slowly walked to it, and smiled as if she was meeting an acquaintance. The auto driver asked her where she wanted to go. The woman replied in her soft, feeble voice, 'I am suffering from a disability and it is very hard for me to get up in the auto all by myself. Could you please get down from your seat and help me get in? Otherwise, I won't be able to make it up to the seat.' This statement confused the driver. How did this old, weak woman get to this road out of nowhere? If she could walk to this place from wherever she came, how did she lack the power to get into the auto? He did not get down from the auto right away but leaving a helpless woman alone after she asked him for help would not sit right with his conscience. As he considered his next move, he noticed that the look in the woman's eyes had changed. She fixed a fierce look on idols and photos of the deities placed in front. The eyes betrayed anger and hatred. She looked back at the driver and bursting out in a shrill laughter, asked him once again to get down from the auto and help her. Her hair was flying around despite there being no wind and her laughter gradually became hysterical. The driver said a prayer to the idols of gods and goddesses and sped ahead. They were his only bet on staying alive. He stopped when he reached a populated market, he was panting in anxiety and his heart was racing. He felt that he had closely escaped death. His faith increased indefinitely as he realized that the old woman was nothing but an evil spirit who could not get in his vehicle due to the placement of those idols and photos.

The public perception of such experiences depends on the number of people who face them. If just one person reports a horror incident, it is often assumed that the person was hallucinating or making it up. In this case too, people have attempted to deny the claims of the auto driver as well as the other people who shared similar experiences while travelling alone on this road. But this notion of the existence of supernatural spirits has remained well attached to this place. This winding road covered in the shadow of the trees, with a crematorium and graveyard nearby, has every necessary element for scary stories. Once you know a few of them, you would also want to avoid going down this road in the evening.

21

VICTORY THEATRE

Have you ever watched a movie in a vacant movie theatre? Even after your eyes adjust to the dark, it is still difficult to identify the person sitting right beside you when the only light present is one from the screen. There are a few whispers and the sounds of chairs being adjusted but no faces can be discerned in the pitch-black of the hall. A movie theatre with such an ambience is a common place to be feared. One such famous place is the Victory Theatre in Pune.

Single screen movie theatres are gradually going extinct and Victory Theatre is one of the oldest single screen movie theatres in Pune. This theatre has a long history and seems to be doing well still. It was established when India was still under British rule on the East Road in Pune Cantonment, also known as the Pune Camp. This cinema hall was founded with the name 'Capitol'. The owners of this theatre had a prolonged legal battle against a leading multiplex-chain about the rights for this property and after winning the suit in 1987, they changed its name from 'Capitol' to 'Victory'. The Capitol Theatre withstood a bombing attack by the revolutionaries of the Indian independence movement on 24 January 1943. This bombing had killed four Englishmen and injured eighteen other people.

Not much has changed about this movie theatre. The exterior has been kept almost intact, a bit of modernization has been done to the interior, the projection system has also been upgraded to enable the screening of 3D movies, and an air conditioning system has been installed. The touch of British colonialism has remained everywhere in the Pune Cantonment, this hall is no exception. The vintage theatre still has a balcony and stall seating arrangements as was the norm in the past. The building has high ceilings, supported by strong wooden rafters, arches in the front, and delicately decorated pillars. The Pune Cantonment was built in 1817 as a stronghold of the armed forces of the-then government, and Capitol Theatre was one of the entertainment venues dedicated to the army. In the old times, various plays used to be staged here.

There are many haunted places in Pune but due to the large footfall at movie theatres, Victory Theatre has become one of the most popular ones. People often come here out of curiosity, as it is easily accessible and fairly affordable. Biplab was one such person. Biplab came to Pune for his IT job a few years ago and had stayed since. He had read about this theatre on some blogs and social media posts and decided to visit. The theatre is not among the modern-day luxuries, and neither is it situated in any shopping mall. There were very few people in the audience on a weekday evening. The ticket was pretty cheap and a stubborn Biplab sat on a middle seat in a middle row, determined that he was not scared of anything.

Once the movie started, he looked around and counted the number of people in there. There were not more than five people in the hall. A few minutes later, probably a couple of them exited the hall. Biplab was feeling a bit uneasy. He reasoned that the feeling was probably because of all the stories that he had heard about this hall. He felt uncomfortable and kept looking back time and again. Did someone get up from their chair again? Biplab thought he heard someone getting up. He turned around to look, there was no one there. There were still two or three people in the audience, nothing to be afraid of.

Biplab tried to focus on the movie instead. Was that a laugh? He clearly heard someone giggling in the back. Although, there was nothing funny about the movie. They were probably gossiping among themselves. That laughter had seemed a bit unusual. Biplab thought he was overthinking. Turning back to the screen, he saw a shadow, someone was covering the projector. He looked back again in annoyance. Still, there was nobody to be seen. What a suffocating situation! It was not even an hour since the movie had started. He thought he should assess if other people felt the same way before leaving the theatre. Biplab got up from his seat and walked up and down the aisle. He could shift to a better seat, he thought. He was surprised to see that the hall was completely empty. Not a single person was watching the movie with him. Was he alone? What happened to those two or three people he saw entering the hall? He remembered a couple of them had left, but where were the others? Were those just shadows of other people? Biplab took his phone out of his pocket to turn on the flashlight and check for other viewers. The phone was running out of battery. Once again, he heard someone getting up from a chair in the front row. He turned again to find nobody. Again, the same sound, as if someone was hurriedly trying to get up from their seat. Biplab turned on the flashlight. He was starting to freak out and decided it was time to get out. It was really suffocating there. He was walking towards the exit door when he heard the same sound again, this time from the seat left of him. A chill ran down his spine. Was there someone invisible standing just beside him? He sensed someone breathing on his shoulder. He started running to get out of the hall but couldn't find an exit. He was surrounded by walls! He ran around the hall but could not spot a single entry or exit door anywhere. His whole body was starting to feel cold, he began shivering and sweating at the same time, and his throat had gone dry…was he trapped in this haunted place? With immense effort, he tried to calm himself and stood still for a moment. He could hear loud laughter and the sense of someone standing right behind him.

'Hey you, get up! The movie has ended.... Hey mister!'

Biplab was startled out of sleep. The lights were on. A maintenance guy was waking him up. He stared at the man. What happened just a few minutes ago? Should he tell this guy? The man spoke again, 'Let's go sir, it's time to head home'. Biplab got up from his seat and looked around the hall once again...it couldn't have been a dream. It just couldn't!

Coming out of the theatre, he stepped into the crowd and felt relieved after seeing so many normal people. Biplab realized he was trapped in a strange timeline with no exit. How could he share the experience he just had? Could he have experienced so many things in a short nap? Arranging his scattered thoughts, he took out the phone from his pocket to check the time. The phone was pretty hot. He turned it back to find that the flashlight was on! Wasn't he running around the closed theatre with his phone's flashlight in that *dream*?

22

NATIONAL LIBRARY

One of the most intriguing aspects of any metropolitan city is that you can always find a moment of silence in the deafening cacophony. On the south bank of the river Ganga, passing through the crowded streets, once you cross the huge iron gate of Kolkata National Library, you immediately feel as if time has turned back. The vintage Victorian structure of the white building, muffled from the noise of the surrounding streets by thick rows of trees, offers a piece of silence in the middle of Kolkata.

The soothing smell of old books hangs around inside this huge library. Apart from the old fans hanging from the high ceilings, the only other sound to be heard is the ruffling of pages or the gentle thud of books. However, the long empty corridors in between huge bookshelves sometimes give a strange sensation. The place closes down just around dusk.

The last person to leave the huge halls often turns around wondering if they heard something that does not exist. The old books might hold all the mysteries of the world, but this building itself stands as evidence of the many tricks of time.

Beerbahadur, a night guard at the museum, had witnessed something strange one night. As he finished his duty he saw an episode from history played right in front of his eyes, a history that spilled blood on that very ground of the library, which was not exactly a library at that time. This building has had many names and many inhabitants over time. If we just follow the chain of names this building had, we can get a sequence of the events that took place here. Around the eighteenth century, this place was a part of the Belvedere Estate. The nawab of West Bengal, Mir Jafar, was the resident of the estate along with his beautiful young wife. Bengal was under the jurisdiction of the East India Company during those days and the first Governor General of Bengal, Warren Hastings, grew close to this nawab. Hastings didn't need long to figure out the gaps in the relationship between the nawab and his wife, Mani Begum. He got to know the lady and made frequent visits to the estate. Not long after, the begum appealed to Hastings for a mahal of her own to have some time for herself and her prayers. The mahal was built shortly afterwards and became the Khaas Mahal of the begum. Naturally, there was no longer any restriction on Hastings visiting her on a regular basis. The nawab wasn't aware of the situation till he paid a surprise visit to his wife, and found her being intimate with the governor general. The nawab couldn't do much since he was serving the East India Company at that time. He had to hand over the estate to Hastings and leave the place. The building gradually adopted the British aesthetic, overcoming its Nawabi demeanour, with the new name Hasting's House. Its story started getting bloody after that.

Hastings had been in a relationship with Baroness Von Imhoff, the lady with whom he had returned from England after a scandal. However, his legal officer, Philip Francis, took advantage of the governor's busy schedule and became close to the baroness. He kept visiting her in her room and a loyal servant of the house informed the baron, her husband. Francis had a close save but he couldn't keep it a secret any longer. This scandal affected Hastings more than the baron. He challenged Francis to a duel.

On a December night, it started as a game following the rules on the western grounds of Hasting's House. They despised each other politically as well as personally, but they probably didn't want to take it any further than a duel that night. However, their rivalry over the baroness got the better of them. Francis was shot in the neck. Hastings, along with all other witnesses, hurried to the aid of Francis. The governor even arranged for a palki, a carriage to take him to the hospital. It was a night of full tide on the old Ganges River. Francis had lost too much blood by then and struggled for his last breath inside the palki. He couldn't make it to the hospital and died right there.

When Beerbahadur, the night guard of the present-day National Library was crossing the western lawn on the night of the full moon, he saw the palki crossing the grounds. He saw the pale young man, covered in blood, lying inside the carriage. His hand was dangling from the carriage door, leaving a trail of blood on its way. He saw the carriage and its misfortune disappear into the moonlight.

Once in a while, the readers who visit this place get distracted by the sound of a heavy carriage. The building has kept its secrets well hidden from those puzzled eyes and savoured the interest that people showed in its past.

23

THE OFFICE IN KOLKATA

The long period of Covid lockdowns has produced two types of employees, one who feels uneasy confined to their work from home desks without the chaos of a giant office and the other who is praying that they never have to visit an office building everyday again. Some employees discuss plans for when the office would reopen and the fun they are missing, and some people complain about the excessive amount of work they are needing to put in to complete their tasks while work from home norms are in place. On a fine weekend a bunch of work friends had gathered on the rooftop of a colleague's house. They had travelled from the nearby cities. They were meeting after ages as they barely got a chance to be in the same city since offices started operating remotely. Probably the norms of keeping a social distance has brought real friends a bit closer in a way. Joy was talking about the distant lights and noises coming from the nearby subway route, the water logging in Kolkata city, and gradually came to the story of the MNC office where he used to work.

As it got late, the stories took a turn towards experiences of loneliness and boredom and landed on the fear of people who live alone. The fear that gathers in the mind from living a lonely life in a remote location devoid of social interaction begins with a feeling of irritation and turns into a fear, leading to beliefs about the existence of ghosts around. While exchanging different experiences among friends, Joy brought up the long time he spent without seeing his office and remembered a very popular ghost story about it. The tale is not a secret, quite a few newspapers have published articles about it and nearly all the employees of the office know about it. The speculation and gossip about the existence of a supernatural entity at an IT hub, which is in some ways an institute representing the advancement of science and technology, is endless! The third floor of Tower 3 in the Kolkata MNC's office has long remained a place that is feared by the employees and a lot of other people who regularly need to visit that building or are around it at night. A group of friends became very keen to know all that Joy had to share about it. Joy began to narrate his experience from half a decade ago in that office.

It was a winter evening. Most of the office employees had left for the day and some of them were still working towards finishing their assignments. There were barely any people remaining on the floor, there was a little more to do before he too would leave the office. It was not very easy to bring tasks back home with them as it used to be with work from home norms. Time was slowly passing while spending time squinting at the bright desktop display in his cubicle. After a bit he felt that someone else walked into the office. There were a couple more people working in different cubicles; he did not pay much attention as anyone could come up to check what he was working on. Joy was deeply involved in the task at hand, he did not get a chance to turn around and chat with the guest at his workspace. Some time passed. Joy was slightly annoyed as the task was taking too long, no matter how he tried to solve the bug. He was sensing that someone else was in his workspace, wandering nearby, but he was not certain about who and where that person was. Suddenly, he felt someone was leaning over him and looking at the screen. He felt a breath on his neck and shoulder. He turned around but there was nobody to be seen. Getting back at his screen, he saw the screen was covered by a strange black shadow. He sensed danger and stopped whatever he was doing at that very moment. He got up, pushed the power button on the computer and walked out of the room. He passed a few days thinking that he was saved from imminent danger that day, but he was still doubtful about whether there was actually anybody present in his cubicle or looking at the screen over his shoulder or if he was just hallucinating due to the fatigue. He tried to gather his friends in the office so that he would not be almost alone on the floor after late in the evening, or he tried his best to complete the tasks as soon as possible to avoid staying after regular working hours.

Few months passed without any other strange events. Once again, he was stuck with an important project after work and he was hurrying to get it over with as fast as possible. After completing the agenda, he got up to visit the restroom once before starting his commute towards home. On his way to the lavatory, he crossed a janitor cleaning the floor with an unusually long broom. Joy went in, got refreshed and splashed water on his eyes and face and came out. The janitor had vanished. If the guy had proceeded towards the balcony, he would have spotted him, and if he began cleaning the hallway and went towards the workspaces then he would be right in Joy's line of sight. But the place was empty and Joy was the only person there, looking around baffled. The floor too, was strangely dry, even though there was someone cleaning it with disinfectant and water just a moment ago. Where did the janitor go? Joy did not get back to his cubicle. He walked straight to the elevator and pressed the button to the ground floor. He visited the janitors' office and asked if there was anybody assigned to clean the third floor right now. One of the security guards was surprised at this question, but understood the situation in a second and told Joy to immediately leave the office and head home. Joy said he still had a small amount of work left and his bags and belongings were still sitting in his cubicle. The security in-charge called up a few more personnel and requested them to accompany Joy to the third floor. Joy visited his desk, quickly completed the task he had to do, took his bag, and got out with the people who were accompanying him. Later the security in-charge told him that though it was still not something proven, but seeing an unfamiliar face around that floor after the evening was a bad omen that could cause something really dangerous.

The gossip amid that group of friends continued until late that night but most of the following stories were related to the experience that Joy shared. He was not alone, his friends brought up similar stories that they had heard from their other friends working in similar offices. There were rumours about the chairs and tables moving around on their own in this office. Once someone spotted that an empty storeroom was suddenly completely unarranged without any known human intervention, the computers on this floor tend to have black screens and become unresponsive way more than the other places in the campus. With this prolonged period with all the employees working from home, the third floor of Tower 3 of this office has been vacant for a pretty long time. Maybe the shadows have gotten a bit darker by the time. Maybe we will be listening to some more rumours about that place again.

24

THE SPIRIT'S WELL

What if you peeked into a well and the still, motionless water reflected a face that's not yours? Stories of possessed wells are fairly common in rural India. These stories date back several years and some of them have become well known over time. One such story originates in Punjab.

This story is based on Bhagta Bhai Ka, a village that has developed into a town, located in the Bhatinda district of Punjab. This village witnessed a few strange incidents and its well has become an integral part of the stories of this village. Some people believe to this day that there exists some kind of supernatural power in that village and especially in the well. From an outsider's perspective, there is nothing too unusual about this small town, the only thing that stands out is an ancient gurudwara. This place has produced the famous athlete Parduman Singh Brar who took part in the 1954

Asian Games in Manila, and won gold medals in the events of shot put and discus throw, becoming the first Asian athlete to achieve the feat. Bhagta Bhai Ka is also known for producing good quality equipment for industrial farming including harvesting machines, power tillers, modern tractors, etc. But the stories about a well near the old Gurudwara overshadow the tales of modernization and industrial progress in this town. In the local language, the very name of this well is Bhooton Wala Khoo, literally meaning 'The Well of Ghosts'. What is in this well?

The well was dug and built by some supernatural spirit at a time when there was no water well in the entire village. The stories say that Bhai Behlo was given the responsibility of overseeing the construction of a portion of the famous Golden Temple of Amritsar. The quality of the necessary building materials, like bricks and others, depended on him. Observing his dedication towards the work and the quality of the construction that was done under Bhai Behlo's supervision, the fifth Sikh Guru Arjan Dev was very pleased. The guru then requested Bhai Behlo to travel across Punjab and spread the word and wisdom of Sikhism. The successor of Bhai Behlo was Bhai Bhagta. Bhai Bhagta too, was a religious Sikh devotee. People travelled from faraway places to him, seeking solutions to their problems. This village, 'Bhagta Bhai Ka' got its name from this Bhai Bhagta, and the story behind the construction of this water well begins with a person who walked a long way seeking a remedy from Bhai Bhagta about an issue he had.

A government official came to Bhai Bhagta seeking a cure for the illness of his daughter. He hoped to get his daughter completely cured by this renowned devotee. This officer, Diwan Ramu Shah, who had travelled all the way from the distant city of Lahore, said that his daughter was possessed by a spirit and only Bhagta Bhai could save her from the imminent threat. After carefully listening to the officer, Bhagta Bhai cordially helped him and cured the poor girl. Diwan Ramu Shah had given up all hopes before coming here and when he was saved by these miraculous efforts of Bhagta Bhai, he wanted to express his gratitude in some way. Bhagta Bhai did not want to ask for something for his personal gain, instead, he wanted something that would help the entire community. Bhai thought of building a well in the village so that all the villagers would benefit from it. He asked the officer to arrange the necessary bricks and other items for the construction of the well. The officer was more than willing to agree with this demand but he expressed his limitation—that he would not be able to carry all those bricks from his distant residence in Lahore. Meanwhile the preparations for constructing the well had already begun. Seeing the hardship of the villagers and the problem of transferring bricks from such a distance, Bhagta Bhai took the initiative of leading the construction. Bhai told the officer that he should arrange for the goods and that making them reach the village of Bhagta Bhai Ka would be Bhagta Bhai's responsibility. The very next morning, the villagers were surprised to see that not only had all the bricks reached their village, but the construction of the well was almost complete. They would not have to struggle anymore for a pot of potable water, the source was right here. Had the ghost really listened to the requests of Bhagta Bhai and decided to help him and the villagers? The villagers, to this day, feel a great amount of veneration along with a bit of fear, when it comes to this place. A lot of them thought that the water from this well was holy and it could be used for curing many tough diseases. Few of the local people still think that this well is guarded by some devotee spirits who worshipped Bhagta Bhai. Along with the strong religious belief, this well built by ghosts has become a point of curiosity for tourists, people with interest in the history of the nation, and explorers alike.

Since the establishment of Sikhism, this well in the small town of Bhagta Bhai Ka has held a special place among people. This was not built by any human, the ghosts built this entirely over the span of a night after being requested or commanded by Bhagta Bhai. On your way, if you get some time to visit this well in the middle of a hot summer day, maybe you would see someone standing there with you, guarding the well, but not casting a shadow!

25

THE HORROR OF THE SHIVPURI FORT

Shivpuri city is the administrative centre of the district with the same name in the state of Madhya Pradesh. It is also known as Shipri and there are mentions of Shipri in articles related to the emperor Akbar. The emperor used to visit Shipri to hunt elephants. In the sixteenth century, like other main cities and towns of Gwalior, Shivpuri too was a part of the Maratha empire. The power of the Maratha empire began weakening in this region. Later, around the end of the sixteenth century, the Rajput army from the town of Narwar overpowered the Maratha emperor in Shivpuri and got hold of the administration over this region. After a couple of centuries, the Sindhia army had overthrown the Rajput rule under the leadership of Daulat Sindhia. Later, the Sindhias moved their capital to Shivpuri. In the Rebellion of 1857, one of the foremost leaders, Tantia Topi, was killed by the British Government, and the execution of Topi was held in this city.

Shivpuri fort is a famous tourist attraction of this place. Due to its location within the Pohari Tehsil, it is also known as the Pohari fort. The well-decorated walls and beautiful front lawn make this place a popular tourist destination. However, there is a statutory warning that bars the entrance of people to this fort after the sunset. Some inexplicable incidents are the reason that this warning is in place. This fort was built over a couple thousand years ago by the king of Kandarba, some sources also cite the role of the Kachwaha Rajputs in building this fort. Nobody could live in this fort after the Khandarba king. There are rumours that there is a valuable treasure buried deep within the premises of this fort and a spirit roams around here to protect it.

One story goes that a woman came here to prove that with a bit of courage, anyone could spend a night in this fort. From the very next day, this woman began showing some abnormalities in her behaviour. Later, she had to be cured by a religious healer.

Stories of scandal, love, ambushes, and conspiracies build up around royal families and these stories often outlive those families. Such a story regarding the jalsha or the royal dance entertainment of King Veer Khandarba is told till now. A group of supernatural spirits attacked the castle while the residents of this fort were engaged in enjoying the jalsha. Those spirits took over the entire fort and have kept control of it since then. Another tale suggests that King Khandarba's spirit haunts this palace. He was very protective of his riches and his beloved fort. His spirit remained here to guard his belongings, so that nobody could take possession of what he owned once. There have also been a few strange incidents at this fort that have caused the authorities to also declare this place haunted. People have been afraid of this fort for centuries. They have almost completely banned the idea of anyone coming to the fort to spend the night, and they would stop anyone else from doing so. Many people have heard mysterious sounds of song and dance that seemed to be coming from within the Shivpuri fort.

Another event took place in present times. This incident was witnessed by many people and also reported by several news portals. There used to be a school close to the Shivpuri fort. A few miscreant students planned to cheat on their test and they brought some books and notes to hide in this fort. After the exam started, the kids made the excuse of a restroom break and came to the fort to fetch test answers from the books they hid there. Instead of recovering the books and papers they put there, they came across a gory, panic inducing sight. The bunch of panic-stricken kids ran for their lives. Not only that, one of those kids died shortly after the incident. Right after the incident, the horror stories about this place were refreshed. The school later moved to a different location.

Quite a few ghost-busters and people who have a special interest in supernatural spirits have expressed their intention to investigate the myth around this fort. But following numerous accidents occurring in the area, the governing body has prohibited any activity here from evening until daybreak.

Another incident worth mentioning occurred a few years back. Two courageous young lads went into this fort with great enthusiasm about exploring and exposing the 'real' mystery about it. The locals repeatedly warned them about the danger that lay within the gates of the fort and they tried to prevent those kids from entering. Later, the lifeless bodies of those two boys were found. Though we come across many stories about the other haunted places in India, the real occurrence of the incidents and related deaths are not at all common, and Shivpuri fort stands out in this regard.

It could be the unsatisfied spirit of a king guarding his treasure chest, or some other fierce spirit roaming around, or just a group of humans with bad intentions behind the horrific incidents, but the trail of fatal events has never stopped in Shivpuri fort. If you ever enter the premises after dusk, keep your eyes open and ears alert. Danger never announces its approach.

26

THE BONACAUD BUNGALOW

The ghost stories of the mountains have an aura exclusive to them. The remoteness of hills adds to the atmosphere of fear when those stories are told. This story took place in a mountain located in the southern part of India. The part of Western Ghat mountain range which stretches within the state of Kerala is popularly known as the Agasthya mountain range. This range has a peak called Agasthyarkoodam. This 1,868-metre-tall peak is a part of the Agasthyamala biosphere reserve that lies at the border of Kerala and Tamil Nadu. The Agasthya mountain range contains a variety of medicinal plants and this is also the location of the Ponmudi hill station, which is called the Kashmir of Kerala for its scenic beauty. Near Ponmudi hill station, there is the Bonacaud Tea Estate which was established by the British before the independence of India. Tea cultivation is not as prosperous as before, but the fields are still used widely for growing pepper, cardamom, and other spices. Once a well-harvested tea estate and business centre, Bonacaud has now transformed into a basecamp for the trekkers who come to explore Agasthyarkoodam. The mind-blowing natural beauty of this place is enhanced by waterfalls like the Bona falls, Meenmutty falls, Vaduvanchal falls, and many more. The mountain range divides the two states and is decorated with lush green foliage. Taking a walk here, you would hear the sound of distant waterfalls and sometimes even come across a family of elephants walking beside you. Could ghosts really exist here?

This mesmerizing mountain beauty is the site of a horror story from the time of the British Raj. The name of Bonacaud Estate was planned to be Bonaccord, after the French phrase 'Bon Accord', meaning good agreement or good faith. The naming was justified after its establishment in 1850 with efforts from both, the British rulers and the local people. As time passed, a series of saddening events took place here. To push the success of the tea estate, the British people invested a good amount of money and time to rebuild and decorate it. The Sooryakanthi River flowed close to the estate. Due to a lack of foresight, the bungalow was built in an area that lacked sufficient sunlight. The workers frequently fell ill and a lot of them died during their stay. Understanding the issue, the management of the estate decided to move the facility to a lower region on the hill and with the improvement in the health of the remaining workers, the place began to flourish. Many labourers came here from faraway places to find work and some of their families settled in the region. Even now, there are ongoing discussions between the government and the tea estates about their demands, and some of the local residents indicate that the actual reason behind the decline of the tea cultivation here were the supernatural activities and the effects of curses. Apart from the deaths of many labourers during their work, the history of the bungalow still drives chills down the spines of the listeners.

Even after decades, the tale of the Bonacaud Tea Estate bungalow comes up in horror stories exchanged by the fireside among the tourists. There is a well-known story about a lonely kid who wandered around this place. When Bonacaud was renowned for being a point of business and mass cultivation of tea leaves, a young boy, the child of the-then owner of the estate and the overseer of the operations, died. His death remains a mystery to this day. Some people suggest that he was murdered, others say the troubled relationship between the parents of the kid was the primary factor behind his death, and some suggest that a supernatural power was behind his demise. The parents discovered the lifeless body of the boy in the morning. The doctors declared that he had died in the middle of the night. There were clear signs of terror on the face of the corpse. The death of an only child, especially in such mysterious circumstances; there could be no pain greater than this for the parents. They moved out of the bungalow right after this incident, leaving the great property of the tea estate, the lavish bungalow, and went back to England. Their lives had fallen apart. The ownership of the bungalow was juggled around between the British and native businessmen and later it was taken over by the elected government of India. Many springs and winters have passed but the terror of this bungalow has remained the same among the local population. People have spotted a small kid in the window of the building, sometimes even without any person nearby, the shadow of a kid has been seen on the walls. Some have heard a kid screaming for his life. Passers-by have also spotted the glass windows broken without any identifiable force and a child floating around in air. Nobody comes around here after dusk and even if they need to visit this place for some purpose, they try their best to avoid going towards the bungalow. The unhappy soul of the boy who died over a century ago is still roaming around this place haunting the present. This bungalow seems to be stuck in the past, where the occasional sightings of a floating child outside a broken window overpowers all rational minds.

Bonacaud bungalow is one of the places that's nearly ruined by abandonment and the passing of time, a place where the past overshadows the present. There may be a ghost of supernatural power existing there, or maybe not, but you surely can add a little thrill to your trip to Kerala if you decide to give this place a visit and spend some time standing in front of the ruins of this tea estate's ancient bungalow.

27

THE HOTEL IN LONAVALA

'How green and calm the surroundings look during this monsoon! I had only seen this in pictures and in my imagination until today,' Joy exclaimed as Asif drove up the winding mountain route. They had been planning a trip with both of their families for a long time but they were suddenly sent to Lonavala assignment. Their channel had started a new project and they needed new, 'feel good' content. They needed photos and stories of travel that weren't just about where to go and what to eat. The plan was to produce a travel diary. Asif and Joy were pleased to be given the opportunity to photograph the beauty of this hill station during the monsoon rains. Though Lonavala is a familiar place to Mumbaikars, their objective was to write a unique article about the place. They had not planned the trip either. They just hopped in the car without an itinerary for their trip.

A veil of rain was covering the distant hills and the heavy rain fell on the windshield of their car. They were considering the hotels they were passing on the way and Asif was also scrolling some online hotel booking websites on his phone to find a place to stay. He came across a strange link and brought Joy's attention to it. They both had spent a good amount of time researching about the haunted places throughout India. But none of them could believe such a place was located so close to their homes. Not some distant, remote mountain cliffside, but a hotel in a locality in the heart of the Lonavala. A specific room in this hotel was known for paranormal activities. Asif and Joy both decided that there could be no better option to make up a great article for their project. They finalized their stay at this hotel.

Reaching the hotel, they found nothing particularly strange about it. The front desk personnel stated that the specific room was currently out of order due to ongoing construction work and no bookings could be made there. Once they gave a proper introduction of themselves and provided their press identity cards, the hotel representative hinted that the room is not open for booking not just because of the construction, but also due to strange occurrences which they were not allowed to disclose openly. After mentioning the articles they had read on the web that described the unnatural incidents that happened in that room, the guy at the reception desk admitted that many guests had experienced some strange phenomena during their stay in that room. Upon repeated complaints from the guests, the hotel management decided to take no more risks and close that room indefinitely. With help from some contacts, Joy and Asif were finally able to convince the hotel management to let them stay the night in that very room.

The door of this room was unlocked after quite a long time. The staff changed the bedsheets, cleaned the furniture, and sprayed a bit of room freshener to reduce the damp smell the room had acquired over time. The rain was constant; they decided not to go out for the day and take some rest. The hotel staff who came to the room to refill the water jars told them about his own experience. He had felt uncomfortable quite a few times when he walked in through this door. When there were no guests and he had to clean the room, he had felt the presence of someone invisible standing in the corner of the room. He had also spotted the lights of the room randomly flickering at night.

The day passed slowly with the sound of rain in the background and suddenly it was evening. There are not many guests staying in this hotel. They were passing time talking to each other. These two guys were exhausted from their journey and there was nothing to worry about, the dinner would be brought to the room as well. They both began feeling sleepy pretty soon. They decided to put the lights out and take a nap until it was time for dinner.

Some time passed. The room was dark, a thin ray of light came from the lamp lit in the washroom. Joy felt something pulling his ankle. He pulled his leg closer and curled up in his sleep. But then he felt the pull again around both his ankles and his knees. This time his sleep was disturbed and he noticed that something was actually pulling the bedsheet, not his leg. Had Asif woken up and started rearranging the bed? He turned around to find Asif was still fast asleep. Joy sat upright and looked at the end of the bed. It was not a dream, someone had actually pulled the bedsheet as some part of the bedsheet and the blanket were touching the ground now. This could not have happened on its own. Joy returned to his side of the bed but he could not fall asleep right away. He looked around. To his surprise, he spotted a faint blue ray of light near the end of the bed where Asif's leg was. The light was similar to a night lamp. It was not very strong but its range was gradually spreading all over the room. Joy felt a chill run down his spine. He could not spot the source of the light anywhere but the illumination was spreading and getting stronger by time. Joy thought of waking up Asif from his sleep, but there was no response when he called. He almost jumped out in fear, but he held himself down and checked Asif. His breathing was normal but he was not responding at all.

The room was almost entirely lit in that strange blue light; the bedsheet and blankets had nearly been pulled down to the floor. 'Asif! Hey Asif!' still no response from the guy in deep sleep. Being in a state of pure confusion and fear, Joy tried to get down from the bed but he realized he was not able to place his foot on the floor. As if an invisible barrier had been formed around the edge of the cot and he was being prevented from getting out of it. He looked around once again, a faint shadow on the wall was slowly forming the shape of a person.

'Joy! Joy!' Joy was pulled back into consciousness on hearing the call from Asif. He woke up and sat on his side of the bed. Joy looked at Asif. He was clearly visible under the blue light. Asif asked, 'Where is this blue light coming from? I don't remember turning on any blue lamps before sleeping.' Joy could not speak about what he was experiencing till now. The two guys both sat there, staring at each other, filled with fear of the unknown. They had lost track of time, the phone in the room had been ringing continuously for a long time. Asif was the first one to pull himself together. He turned on the flashlight of his phone and picked up the call. There was nobody speaking from the other end of the telephone. Someone began knocking on the door. Joy jumped out of the bed. But again, there was nobody waiting outside the room once the door was opened. Only the blue light seemed to escape from the door in the centre of the room. Asif looked towards Joy and noticed a dark shadow slowly walk out of the room.

Going back to Mumbai, this duo prepared their article, narrating a version of this experience. This is a strange mystery that has stayed confined to this one room of this hotel in Lonavala. If you get a chance, you may decide on visiting this place someday. Maybe you would be the one to find out the source of that strange blue light that Joy and Asif spotted in their room?

28

THE WOMAN OF THE FIRST FLOOR IN YOGESHWARI

We find that the famous haunted places all share a common phenomenon, they all have a large number of people who believe the horror stories related to them. Similar incidents have kept occurring over time and as more and more people experience them, their faith in the existence of the supernatural gets stronger. Their stories keep spreading by the word of mouth, eventually making that place well known. The sleepless city of Mumbai has countless stories like these. Like many other places in Maharashtra, the capital city of Mumbai too, has multiple disturbing and eerie places. Mumbai doesn't sleep at night and just like that phrase, there are many places in Mumbai with stories that will take away the sleep from your eyes for a night or two. One such place is a haunted house in Mumbai's Yogeshwari, specifically the first floor of that house.

There are numerous stories about the first floor of this house among the locals. Between the incidents that have taken place, and the incidents that could have happened, there remains a great deal of difference. The local people say that some incidents had taken place around the first floor of this house which could not be explained by logic. An old woman who lives close to this house, saw a light from the first floor being turned on out of nowhere. The light was glowing continuously for some time and then it suddenly vanished. She looked in that direction out of curiosity. In between the flickers of the light, she had seen something like a shadow in the veranda of the house. Paying a bit more attention, she figured out that a woman was standing in the veranda for a little while. Then that figure from the veranda vanished in thin air. The light went off for the time being and there was nobody around the place. The old woman clearly remembers that she did not see the woman going in or out of the veranda, and the figure just vanished. She tried searching for the woman on the balcony in the following days, but it was all for nothing.

This pink-coloured house, located in a fairly populated colony in the Yogeshwari area, has raised quite a few unanswered questions in the local area. Another resident of the colony had seen a similar figure standing on the roof of this building. She was walking on the rooftop after the evening, and she seemed to sense that someone was looking at her despite not turning around or making eye-contact. As soon as she felt she was being watched, she stopped walking. A faint crying could be heard. Was the girl crying? While the resident was staring at the girl on the roof, she suddenly vanished from there and reappeared on the balcony. Not even a few seconds had passed, how could she shift from one place to the other, climbing down so many stairs in such a short duration? Did she teleport? While the observer was wondering about the possible answers to the questions that were arising one after the other, the faint sound of crying and sobbing reappeared and now, with that sob, there was a hint of a painful groan.

He was surprised once again as the woman vanished from the balcony within the blink of an eye. He looked around that building for traces of her. She was now standing in front of a window inside a room. Her gaze was directed at him, and she kept staring at him. After a few minutes of staring, the woman began fading away. The faint sounds of sobbing and groaning were slowly going further away as she was gradually dissolving into thin air. The guy wondered whether what he saw was just a dream or a creation of his subconscious mind. He looked back after a while. The entire first floor of that pink building was dark, just the way it appeared every single day. What he saw and why he saw all that, he spent the night in search of answers to these questions.

Waking up the next morning, he went out and shared his experience with one of the shopkeepers at a local grocery store. When he finished telling his story, there was a momentary silence. The grocer said that a woman actually used to live on the first floor of that building. She was an air hostess by profession. Her death was a mystery. Many people thought that she was murdered inside that house. After her death, the woman's spirit kept returning to let others know about her existence. Some people have seen her on the balcony, some have seen her on the rooftop. A few have heard the sounds of her crying from the room, and a few people have spotted her pointing to the room she used to live in. Perhaps she was indicating something for others to find out about the gruesome fate she had to meet with.

There is a continuous trend of unnatural deaths creating an atmosphere of fear around either the place where the crime took place or the place the victim used to live in and it gets even stronger in the cases where both these places are the same. Yogeshwari is known for its temples, caves, and other places to roam around on a tour. The suburb of Yogeshwari is especially known for its caves because it was named after those caves. All of these caves were devoted as an offering to the Hindu goddess Jogeshwari or Yogeshwari. After that, the entire place got the name of the goddess who was thought to be the owner of the locality. And in this suburb in the western part of Mumbai, the mysterious death of an air hostess has added a haunting chapter to the story of the metropolitan city.

29

THE GHOST OF THE HIGH COURT

Mr Batakrishna was a stamp vendor. During that time, the area where the stamp vendors of Kolkata High Court used to set up shop became deserted by the evening. Once the office compound is vacated, this huge building is eerily silent. The lawyers and judges were leaving the court compound, the chaotic workday was gradually coming to a calming end, and once again the singing birds were able to raise their voices above the chattering crowd. The stamp vendor Mr Batakrishna was ready to call it a day. As he began to walk along the long veranda out of the premises, he heard someone drinking water from a jug. He was familiar with all the stories about a thirsty haunted soul that searched for water every evening.

There are a lot of stories that lurk around the gossip-rich corners of the high court. To the believers, the high court and dissatisfied ghosts are are an inseparable duo. The stories have gotten more and more detailed as generations of people have passed them down the lane of time. Many people curiously ask those who work around the high court, if they have had any supernatural experiences. The court compound has collected stories for centuries.

There is no proof whether Mr Batakrishna actually saw anybody drinking water, but there is a context behind this story of a thirsty soul roaming around the premises. Poet Tapis had to go met with a very saddening fate right here. The British East India company was against him as he protested against their tyranny. They arrested him and kept him locked up in a cell in the high court compound. Poet Tapis was tried in this court and sentenced to jail. They stopped the supply of food and even potable water to his cell. His body was almost completely emaciated by the end of his life. He was forced to the execution table and hanged to death. The stories about his ghost roaming around the high court premises, searching for water, spread among people. After that evening's experience, Mr Batakrishna lost the courage to stay alone in that place in the evenings.

This is not the only story that lives on within the premises of the Kolkata High Court. There are several generations of stories that keep making the rounds. There is another one story that causes fear among many.

Two co-workers were working their shifts during a winter night. Most of their colleagues went home and a few people still remained to complete some urgent work. As there were very few people, it was natural to be startled by the sound of any footstep or the shadows of any unexpected people who happened to pass by the corridor. Even the clock's ticking seemed too loud. Vajahari Paitandi and Manamohan Ghoshal were working at their desks. It was pitch dark outside. Manamohan was sitting between the light and the pile of files in the room. Before finishing off his work, he went to the restroom. It was late in the night, Vajahari probably thought of something and advised not to use the restroom next to the Judge's Court and use the place beside the wall of their section. Manamohan did not want to go to that place and decided to go to the restroom beside the Judge's Court. His footsteps echoed in the long, dark corridor; ignoring Vajahari's advice was probably not a good idea. But the thought of turning back after walking half of the way felt very cowardly to him. Taking a few steps forward, the faint light that was coming from his workroom dimmed even further. There another sound began coming from far away, it was the ringing of anklets. Two more steps and he spotted two legs, a girl was walking towards him, wearing anklets. The girl had a headless body. His heart skipped a few beats as the girl started walking towards him. He lost the power to move forward. The girl stopped, as if she was not expecting anybody to be there and got startled as well and vanished behind the memorial of Justice Syed Amir Ali. Manamohan was stunned, he had heard about some wandering souls that resided in this court. They really did exist. Manamohan lost his consciousness and fell on the floor.

After quite some time, Vajahari began wondering where his colleague had gone. He stood up from his table and began looking around. Taking a couple of steps in the corridor, he spotted his colleague Manamohan fallen senseless on the floor. But who was with him? A girl was splashing water on his face, trying to wake him up…but the girl had no face, it was just a headless body. A cold sensation ran down Vajahari's arms and legs. The moment the girl spotted him, she vanished. He managed to wake up his colleague somehow and picked him up and they both walked out of the building that instant.

Who was this girl? Many who have worked in the High Court, have heard the ringing of her anklets and a few have also spotted this headless woman. At the end of the nineteenth century, the judge of the high court received a strange application—one prostitute asked her name to be removed from the register of common prostitutes. She showed physical reasons behind this application but what she really wanted was to start a new life after escaping the hellhole. She fell in love with a businessman named Shalikhram. The gorgeous woman, Nistar Raut, had applied through a lawyer to get her name removed from the register. But it was not that easy. The judge tried to influence Nistar but once that plan failed, he began pressurizing Shalikhram. When both of these attempts failed, they used one of the powerful customers of Nistar to accuse Shalikhram and Nistar in a case of robbery. Shalikhram was arrested by the police. Nistar's world turned upside down. Her dream of peace and a family was shattered. The rest of the story is still a mystery. After a few days the police found Nistar's dead body. It was beginning to rot, the corpse's head was missing, and there were a couple of anklets on the legs.

After that incident, the disappointed soul of Nistar remained in the high court compound. Others could hear the sound of her anklets, some could even see her. The legend of a helpless woman who just wanted to get back to a normal life still haunts the high court after many years.

30

THE CURSED HISTORY OF THE TALBEHAT FORT

There is a difference between the things that are happening in our everyday world and the things that have happened in the distant past. The events that happened in history take a different shape with every telling and become famous among people; the places associated with these events become popular too. The numerous haunted places that are located in the state of Uttar Pradesh keep making an appearance in new stories time and again. A lesser-known haunted place in the state is Lalitpur. In Lalitpur district, there is a fort in the village of Talbehat which has a saddening tale. Some incidents that occurred in the fort later have marked this place as a scary destination. Because of the incident that took place in this fort a long time ago, the villagers still pass the day of Akshaya Tritiya as a day of bad omen. Mysterious sounds of crying and sobbing can be heard from the direction of the fort in the dead of the night. Among the experiences shared by the villagers, some have also mentioned hearing screams of agony along with the cries of women, sounds that indicate mistreatment and abuse. Many people are scared of setting foot inside this fort even during the day.

Talbehat fort was built during the first half of the seventeenth century by Bharat Singh, to help supervise the territory under the zamindar Mardan Singh. Mardan Singh was a famous zamindar who was adored by others. He managed to rule over his subjects justly and fought in the battle to protect the motherland from the British. During the Revolution of 1857, the zamindar Mardan Singh joined forces with the ruler of Jhansi, Rani Laxmi Bai. The subjects of Mardan Singh respected him for his bravery and were proud of having Mardan Singh as their ruler, but the ones who knew his story, were equally ashamed because of his father, Prahlad Singh. He had committed a crime so heinous that it cast a shadow on this fort as well as the entire village.

When Mardan Singh was busy fighting in the battle, a special ceremony was arranged in the village for the celebration of Akshaya Tritiya festival. The entire village was in a festive mood. The women of Lalitpur went to the house of the zamindar to collect blessings and donations from the wealthy ruler as per the regional rituals. Among these women, there were seven young girls from the village of Talbehat. Prahlad Singh was in the fort at that time and he fixed his cruel eyes on these seven teenage girls. Later that day, he sent his armed guards and abducted them from the village. His lust had overpowered his senses and he raped all seven girls in the fort. The premises were filled with the helpless screams of these abducted girls. All seven of these girls jumped from the terraces of the Talbehat fort and ended their own lives.

That day, the entire village was consumed by grave sorrow. The locality has still not been able to come out from the shadow of the grief that it had to go through that day. They never could accept the suicide of these seven girls and the unspeakable violence they had to go through that day.

There are paintings of seven women outside this fort today. Mardan Singh was behind this. When he returned from the battleground and came to know what his father had done, he was overwhelmed by shame, anger, and disgust. He hired an artist and asked him to paint seven women outside the fort in Talbehat. The artist painted the figures of seven women on the main entrance of the fort to tell people their story and urge them to bring justice in the society. After that day, the villagers of Talbehat stopped celebrating the day of Akshaya Tritiya, nor did they follow any of the rituals related to the rulers. It has been marked as a day of bad omen, a black day since the occurrence of that incident. Even if someone does not know about this story, they would stop for a moment when they look at the painting of the seven women outside the main gate of the fort. The skilled artist pictured the pain, the cry for help, and embossed them into the eyes of all seven of the women figures in the picture. The painting gives the sense of these women who had to go through the abuse requesting justice, rather than demanding revenge, for what was done to them.

The local people still believe that the spirits of these women roam around inside the premises of Talbehat fort. Their screams of agony slices through the silence of the night. Years' worth of sobs and cries have shrouded the village. To the villagers, this fort remains a monument to a dark event of the past. Generations have come and gone but this horrific chapter from history has remained attached to this fort. The people who know about the fort, often make it a destination to satisfy their curiosity about the supernatural beings. From the villagers, one can come to know about the many misdoings of Prahlad Singh.

In the large state of Uttar Pradesh, if you suddenly find yourself setting foot in Lalitpur then you can look around and maybe find the village of Talbehat. At the edge of the village you would find the large and lonely Talbehat fort enduring the elements of nature. The fort that was built keeping great purposes in mind, it still stands alone, seeking justice for the seven young girls.

31

LAMBI DEHAR MINES

Mussoorie, the queen of the hills, is one of the top tourist destinations in India. Located in these beautiful mountains, are places like Kempty falls, Lal Tibba, Gun Hill Point, Mussoorie lake, and a lot more. The beauty of this hill station attracts people from around the country. The town was established by the British officials to help with their operations. In the year 1825, the British army officer Captain Young established this town in the cradle of the mountains. The captain was accompanied by Mr Shore and after the establishment of the town, Mussoorie became their go-to destination for shooting games. Being an old hill town, Mussoorie has a lot of stories of its own. This town is the starting point of the shadowy Garhwal Himalaya mountain range.

Being an old town, some of the old hotels, old houses, and mansions are the setting for many horror stories. A sorrowful tale in the history of Mussoorie emerges from the Lambi Dehar mines. The place with a wailing history and a place where people are still afraid of going. The Lambi Dehar mines used to be abuzz with the noises of people on busy days thirty years ago. Thousands of miners used to work in this limestone mine. The place, located just ten kilometres away from the Mall Road of Mussoorie, sits dead silent on a Monday morning nowadays, carrying horrific stories instead. The truthfulness of the rumours and the stories may not be verified, but the incidents that started everything would definitely haunt the listeners. Nearly fifty thousand laborers who worked here suffered a slow and painful death. The death of so many people in such a short span of time terrified people. Perhaps the conditions in the limestone mine caused severe lung disease among the workers. The air of the mine filled with limestone dust went into their bodies. Their lungs got infected. And with that, a deadly cough began. After the cough started, in a short span of time, blood began appearing with each of those painful coughs. One by one, those affected workers' lives ended in acute pain and breathlessness. This mine that provided a job to thousands of people gradually became a death hole surrounded by the heartbreaking sounds of coughing, crying, and painful screams. After this incident of mass death, the Lambi Dehar mines were completely shut down.

There are countless stories of cursed occurrences around this place and all of them originate from that incident. In the dead of the night, people can still hear wails of the people who died, gasping for air. There are some spirits who roam around at night, pleading for a sip of water, and sobbing between coughs. Many people think that the deadly incident left a permanent mark on the popular imagination, leading to these tales and the associated fear. And some people believe these incidents happen even now, that the spirits of the helpless miners still roam around in the mines.

Horror enthusiasts have not left this place alone. Paranormal explorers and ghost hunters count this mine as an interesting location to explore. Can people really hear the sounds of wailing and crying of the miners in the darkness of the mines? Are there some unspoken messages hidden within their cries? To get the answers, you would need to visit Lambi Dehar mines at night.

32

CHARLEVILLE MANSION

Ghost stories are abundant but we rarely come across a story that tells us about any supernatural spirit who takes pleasure in striking panic among visitors. By 'special type' the indication is toward the spirits. Such spirits could be fundamentally different from others in terms of their appearance, type, their method of inducing fear, and the possible goal they want to achieve by scaring people away. Ghost stories are largely based on their location and its history and the mindset of the people in that area. Shimla is another hill station with a host of mysteries and horror stories. Like Tunnel Number 33 in Barog, the Charleville Mansion in Shimla is a place that retains the uncanny feeling of the past. The mansion stands out because of the horror people experienced here. It is said to be infested by a different kind of spirit called the poltergeist. The concept of a poltergeist spirit originated in Germany. The primary motive of this spirit is said to be disturbing the residents of a house or a locality. Their method of annoying people is to make loud, annoying sounds by throwing utensils and furniture in the house and making strange noises to force the residents out.

The haunted house, Charleville Mansion is a short walking distance away from this Scandal Point crossroads. The name of this mansion is mentioned in the legendary litterateur and journalist Rudyard Kipling's 'My Own True Ghost Story'. Shimla was the city of choice for the officers who came to India to oversee the development and expansion of the railway during the time of British rule. The armed forces also halted in several barracks located across this city and its surroundings. The story of this mansion came from an army officer who chose this place to stay. He had heard some rumours about some paranormal activities in this house but he reasoned that these were being spread by competitors to drive away possible tenants. A couple of days after he moved in, he began hearing strange noises coming from the first floor. He thought some miscreants were making these to drive him out of the place. Determined to punish them, he hung a lock on the entrance to the first-floor rooms. But, after locking the floor, the sounds became louder and more frequent. The officer went up to check one day and unlocking the door, he saw the entire floor was filled with scattered furniture and the big mirror was completely shattered. He moved out of that mansion as fast as he could.

When the First World War was brewing, a British officer

who went by the name of Victor Bailey was deputed to Shimla. He came to this city with his family in the year 1913. The assistant secretary of the Indian Railway Board chose Charleville Mansion to stay with his family as he got it for a very cheap rent. There were rumours about all the previous tenants being driven out of the mansion by the disturbance of the ghosts. Victor and his wife stayed happily in this place, they also hired a person for domestic help who regularly visited to do their chores. But after getting to know about the rumours and the poltergeist activities, Victor got suspicious about the supernatural activities around the building. They had not experienced anything unnatural yet. Being afraid of the unknown, Victor had already put a lock on that one room on the first-floor that was known to be hosting most of the mischievous activities and noises.

Experiencing no interference from the rent-free invisible residents of the mansion, the slight doubt that occurred in Victor Bailey's mind was eased. A few months passed peacefully like that. One fine day, the officer went out with his wife to a dinner party. The house help was working alone and waiting for their return. He suddenly felt like someone was standing on the upstairs floor. When he approached to check what was going on, a series of noises started coming from the first floor. The noises were of hitting furniture with blunt objects, throwing wooden items across the room, and dragging heavy objects on the floor. He was pretty frightened. Looking up once again, he sensed as if a white shadow suddenly moved from the staircase and passed through the locked door. He could not gather enough courage to go upstairs to explore. When the officer returned with his wife, he reported the entire experience to him. Victor and his wife decided to move out of the place after that.

Poltergeists are known for making noises, throwing silverware, utensils and furniture, and ultimately making the place undesirable for living. In today's time, people avoid choosing this mansion over anything else, even before having to experience any such supernatural activity. The aura of horror has remained till this day.

There are stories that suggest a British woman who lived alone in this mansion as a tenant for a few years after Victor Bailey and his wife moved out too. There are no further details available on that woman or whether she had any similar experiences or not. Later, decades after that woman moved out of this place, an Indian took responsibility of this mansion and proceeded to renovate and redecorate the entire thing.

The tales about the existence of poltergeist spirits have remained around this one mansion located in Shimla. A rational mind would always reason that the activities like making sounds, breaking furniture, and driving out tenants from a house, would be something that mischievous humans would do, not some haunted spirit. Though people claim that the aura of horror has drastically reduced after the renovation of this property, this mansion has remained one of its kind, surrounded by the historical rumours and the mysteries. The site of a unique horror story that blends European and Indian traditions.

33

DEV'S ARCADE IN NASIK

Nasik is one of the largest cities in Maharashtra. Situated along the banks of the river Godavari, the city Nasik is also considered holy by a lot of people. It is a destination for many people for their celebration of Kumbh Mela. During this grand festival and fair that is held once every twelve years, tens of millions of people travel to this city. Parallel to being known as a religious place, Nasik is also host to a good number of wineries, that produce a huge amount of wine on a regular basis. A majority of the wine production of the Indian subcontinent is from Nasik. This city is also significant for its automobile production factories.

Shuffling through the tales from the long past to the present-day, we find a variety of haunted locations in Nasik. Ghost hunter groups have also contributed to expanding this list of locations. Among the supernatural hotspots of Nasik, the one place that caught our attention was a place called Dev's Arcade. Located in Sant Kabir Nagar, inside the premises of Veer Savarkar Nagar of Nasik, this place was inaugurated as the first mini shopping mall in the city. But as time passed, its sudden closure, and the experiences of many people who visited this mall has made it famous as a haunted place. Being the first arcade in the city, it first introduced the model of hosting various kinds of stores and shops in one building in the locality. It became well known among the people living in the city but it was suddenly shut down. Why this well planned and fairly flourishing business centre closed its doors all out of a sudden has sparked a lot of debates. Some people say that the owner of the mall was being unable to repay the loan taken from the bank for building the place and the bank proceeded to seize the property, some claim that there is a legal case going on with the mall and its operations are halted till the result of the case is announced, and a group of people believe that there is some kind of supernatural spirit residing in the shopping mall is the actual reason why the regular business of the mall was being hampered.

Opening their shops in this mall had been a big step for many business owners. Many shopkeepers inside the mall had felt the presence of some kind of supernatural entity in their vicinity and they started moving out from the mall after some mishaps. A couple of stores remained operational on the ground floor of this semi-closed shopping mall. Those shops were owned by a single person. The only other person in the mall was the security guard. They tried to stop anyone from entering this building in the evening and strictly warned people against accessing the third floor at any time of the day. Despite the warnings, some people still went inside the mall. They either fainted after stepping in or saw something gruesome and fear-striking after reaching the third floor.

The silence of this abandoned building creates an eerie atmosphere—the posters on the walls and the signboards on top of long-closed shops remain as they were before. Few loose papers have fallen here and there and the discarded furniture is scattered on the floors. A couple of people, claiming to be paranormal researchers, demanded to get inside the closed arcade to research and find out whether any paranormal activity was really going on there or if the entire thing was just a hoax. They had managed to obtain permissions from various authorities to spend the night inside the premises. The locals had repeatedly warned them about the building and asked them to drop the idea of spending a night inside. Their safety was more important than investigating any ghost activity there. However, they ignored all warnings and insisted on staying the night.

They came with their equipment, including cameras. If they really experienced the existence of something paranormal, they would keep a record in photographs as well as in audio recordings. This place was built to host hundreds of people and without any visitors, this place had a creepy atmosphere. The silence was getting denser and scarier by the hour. The point of proving nothing unnatural existed here was more important than encountering something unexpected. They kept the camera turned on, facing the stairs. Losing track of time and tired from the whole day's journey, the two people fell asleep. Their sleep was disturbed by a sudden noise. They got up and looked around, but there was nothing to be seen and then they started noticing the camera footage. There was nothing identifiable for a long duration of the footage but after a certain point, there were some random lights flickering and some strange hissing sounds. Zooming in on the footage, it could be determined that a group of people was trying to get up the stairs while holding a flashlight in their hand. The sound was coming from those people whispering among themselves. The two were now alert and positioned the camera at the same spot, facing the same direction. They were determined not to fall asleep again.

They were woken up by some of the locals who were visibly anxious. They had appeared unconscious. This phenomenon is not new for this place. Many people who came to explore the supernatural activities here were later found unconscious. Hastily getting up, the two researchers began browsing through the recordings of the camera from the previous night. The entire footage remained intact, the only part that was missing was the portion where they had seen those lights and voices last night. It was very strange. No one could trim a specific part of a video without removing the storage of the camera. If they really even wanted to erase the footage, those people could delete the whole video, but surprisingly the rest of the video was intact. Even if someone had done that, going through all the trouble of removing the storage, editing out the video and restoring it, they would have woken up from the noise of it. They were in such deep sleep that the people had to sprinkle water on their faces and shake their bodies to wake them up. They did not eat any food from any stranger, so the chance of intoxication was very low, then what could be the reason for such deep sleep? The answers to these questions are not known by anyone.

Many shopping malls and market complexes are famous for their uniqueness but Dev's Arcade in Nasik is famous for being a haunted place. The first arcade of the entire city that has been abandoned for decades.

34

MADRAS CHRISTIAN COLLEGE

There are various types of stories which are frequently associated with educational institutes like colleges and universities. Thousands of pupils come in every year to study, to progress towards achieving their dreams, and they graduate after completing their education. The unspoken stories remain scattered across classrooms, corridors, canteens, libraries, and reading rooms. The primary difference between workplaces and educational institutes is that unlike workplaces, the faces around the campus change every year and the characters in the story are more numerous and diverse. Every institute has their own sad stories, funny tales, and gossips with a bit of both. Madras Christian College's story has an element of fear that stands out from regular ghost stories. This college is situated in Tambaram East in the district of Chengalpattu in Tamil Nadu. Tambaram lies close to the highway connecting

Chennai and Trichy. This college is pretty old and it has gathered a lot of strange stories over time.

Reverend John Anderson was one of the Christian missionaries who came to India from Scotland. In 1837, he established the General Assembly School, which was later developed into this college. He had a significant impact in the spread of the study of the English language and development of general educational infrastructure across southern India. This government-sponsored college operates under the University of Madras. After a century of the college's establishment, the Tambaram Conference was held here. Tambaram Conference was the Third World Missional Conference and after the event, the World Council of Churches was established. Madras Christian College is known across the country for its high standard of education.

People with a keen interest in paranormal activities, supernatural events, unexplained mysteries, maintain that most of the ghost stories that are famous are not based around some historical establishment, but around residences or somewhere an unnatural death occurred.

The Madras Christian College has a sad backstory. A student took his own life after facing a rejection. After his death his soul did not let go of the place so easily. Even to this day, it lets others know about its presence through several incidents on campus. A strange emptiness can be felt around the laboratories and libraries of this campus. These calm rooms with the aroma of the aging pages hold the memories from years of people coming in and going out.

Their presence remains with the lab instruments and the pages of the books. One of the laboratories of this college, too, has a story telling us about someone from the past. You can hear someone speaking very softly if you walk in here at night, and if you pay more attention, you will hear someone is reading out from a book. If you enter the room and try to locate the source of the voice, the sound stops. Perhaps that avid reader feels disturbed in the presence of somebody else. If you still continue to look around, you will find nobody else in the room. The old lamps dimly light up the area in the dark of the night. A lot of people had held bets and visited this place, but none of them could stay for long, they all fled in fear.

Pupils in this college have heard sudden footsteps in the empty corridors at night, they have witnessed water faucets open right after they have come out of the washroom having closed them. Noticing the lights flickering in classrooms or restrooms, people tried to run out of these places and suddenly felt someone standing behind them. There are several trees and plants across the campus, some wild animals also roam around. In the half-dark, half-lit dusk people were scared of deer jumping around in the foliage and some of them spotted a strange creature who was half-deer, half-human.

People tend to develop rigid beliefs from repeatedly listening to stories and gossips. They begin to perceive normal events as paranormal. The experience of a young student from this college is not that kind of mistake. He was about to walk home after his day, but he could not leave the campus. The guy kept walking for a long time but every time he would find himself at the same spot where he started from. It is not like he lost the direction of the road, every time he tried to take a step forward, he felt someone was there, someone about to grab him from behind. When he turned around, he saw no one. So much time had passed in a situation like this, he lost track of it. After a while, he found a big relief after spotting a few more people were heading that way. Since then, he never dared walking down that lane.

It is debatable whether the ghost of the student who committed suicide after being rejected on his proposal in Herbert Hall is still roaming around campus at this well-known college. People with weak hearts get scared when things happen suddenly, like furniture falling and rolling over on its own or loud laughter. Roaming around the campus, you'll find the room number 148 is locked. Situated opposite Herbert Hall, this is the room which witnessed the death.

Every year new sets of students come in and the older batch of pupils graduate, but these balconies, libraries, laboratories, restrooms retain the history of all the shadows of the people who passed by.

35

THE LIFT IN THE UNIVERSITY CAMPUS

The difference between the day and the night becomes quite prominent inside the premises of large educational institutes. Every place on campus, the classrooms, corridors, the canteen, hums with people's talks and laughs but at the end of the day when the lectures end, everything falls eerily silent. The footsteps of someone walking in a distant corridor become distractingly noisy. Many educational institutes in India have horror stories associated with them, and these stories are frequently shared as gossip. This institute is not too old, but even in this short span of time, some supernatural activities have made it a topic of discussion frequently. This institute, offers engineering, management, and pharmacy courses. It is located in Nigam Nagar in Ahmedabad. Located in the heart of the busy Ahmedabad city, it is beautiful campus carpeted by the well-trimmed grass. It wouldn't cross one's mind even once that there could be such a story within these modern buildings. The experience of one of the staff members of this university was the source of the rumour that spread throughout the campus and beyond. The effect the event had on him also scared a lot of people. This was not an isolated incident, there have been a few more times when people have encountered something extraordinary, something supernatural in this campus. Taking the lift to the upper floors, students and staff sometimes feel as if someone is in the lift with them, despite there not being a single person sharing the lift. Sometimes, the lift stops suddenly while moving, the gates open even if there is nobody getting in or out, without anyone pressing the buttons. The furniture in the corridors suddenly relocates itself, sometimes they get tumbled around by some mysterious power. Some windows open and close with loud bangs and the lights flickered throughout the floors. In the crowd of these small incidents, the experience of that staff member is the one that binds the other stories together.

The campus is located in a lively city, but the environment becomes quite calm and lonely after the busy day comes to an end. A staff of the university walked towards the lift in the evening. There was nobody remaining to take the lift from the lower floors. As he walked in the lift and proceeded to press the button to his destination, another woman walked in. She was not one of the university's teachers or staff, and he could not recall seeing her face before. Where was she going this evening after all the official operations had closed for the day? He still had not pressed any button, but as he felt a bit uneasy about asking her where she would go, he selected his own destination floor. Lifting up his head, he was a little surprised looking at her again. The lift had started moving and she was staring at him with a strange look. The eyes had a fierce aggression and she had a slight smile forming at the corner of her lips. The interior of the lift started to feel very suffocating. The woman was not blinking at all. It seemed like she took a step forward towards him. He was stuck in the corner, why was the lift taking so long to reach? There was a strange sound coming from the lift, like a predator growling at its prey. The woman was still smiling from the corner of her lips, but now there was blood dripping from her mouth. The lift stopped moving with a loud noise, as if it hit the roof. As soon as the door opened, he jumped out from the lift to the floor. Before he could even gather the strength to scream, the doors of the lift closed and as the lift started to move again, a loud laughter became audible from there. Where did she go by the lift? He was not in a state to think and investigate what happened after this. He gathered whatever strength he had left and walked away from that place. Luckily, he found a couple more teachers who were still working in the building, but his shivering body was on the verge of unconsciousness from the exhaustion he had gone through.

The people on the campus saw drastic changes in the man's behaviour after this dreadful day. Whenever he tried to talk to anybody or if someone went to him to ask anything, he would stutter and lose track of what he was saying. He could not eat anything for a few days as well. Seeing someone from the staff behave weirdly raised a few eyebrows, many people started looking into the reason behind this. But the incident had taken place in such a time of the day that nobody had any proper information about what happened. So, nobody could establish the truthfulness of what he was saying at that time. Ultimately, the doctors advised him to go through a treatment for mental illness. But those people who had seen the look in his eyes for the few days after the incident, understood that the man had seen something so horrible that it could not be the doing of some earthly creature. The students and employees have turned their heads to look when they hear sudden noises of water droplets dripping from the faucets around the classrooms, laboratories, and washrooms, despite knowing that they would not see anyone around. The fear of suddenly witnessing something gruesome and terrifying has spread across the campus along with the experience shared by that staff who came across the strange woman in the lift. In spite of being one of the most successful universities for technology and science, this place hosts the fear of the supernatural behind a wall of scientific rationalism and declinations. People still think twice before taking the lift alone after the daylight dims.

36

THE HOTEL ON THE HILL

There are countless ghost stories surrounding hotels, inns, and resorts. They consist of rooms where various types of people come from different places with their unique kinds of happiness and sorrow. Each of these sets of four walls witnesses new people with their new stories every day. There is a superstition that a place where a horror movie is shot is bound to host some kind of supernatural activity in the future. The people who are connected to the particular movie, or someone in their families would surely experience something that can't be explained with logic. Perhaps they are just coincidences but some weird stuff has happened with the movie sets arranged for scary movies throughout the world. There is an abundance of tales of supernatural occurrences on movie sets. Many people also claim that these are rumours spread by the stakeholders of the movie, a trick to create more publicity. A lot of these experiences were quite frightening. During the shooting of a renowned Hindi film *Jagat*, the artists witnessed a scary incident while shooting in a beautiful hotel in Ooty. A well-known dancer was staying in this hotel with their dance troop and they heard loud sounds of dragging heavy furniture on the upper floor of their rooms. They tried reaching the reception over the phone but that would refuse to connect too. Later, the hotel staff told them that there were, in fact, no rooms on the floor above them. When the news media shed light upon this story, this hotel, which was already known for having some unexplainable incidents, became the talk of the town once again.

Udhagamandalam or Ootacamund, Ooty in short, is a place for mountain lovers. It is a popular destination for tourists around the Nilgiris Hills in Tamil Nadu. Ooty is also known for its great quality tea. A lot of people visit Ooty just to experience the various types of flavours and aromas of the tea produced in this city. Apart from these, the other popular places include the Botanical Garden, Ooty Lake, the majestic garden of roses, and some gorgeous hills. With increasing interest from tourists, the business of short-term rentals has also grown. Ooty hosts a lot of well decorated and lavish hotels. This hotel on the hill too, is one of those eye-soothing, professionally decorated hotels in this city.

The Maharaja of Mysore or Mysuru was the one behind the construction of this hotel. He built this as a place to spend the summer in 1844. Later, as time passed, it was transformed into a posh hotel. Though built by the king of Mysore, it really began flourishing as it became one of the primary stays to the high net-worth individuals during the British Raj. The premises cover a huge amount of land, and keeping the building in the centre, a rich green foliage beautifies the surroundings. And in parallel with this beauty, there is an uncanny fear about this holiday home.

It is not just a few famous people whose stay lasted a few days, the hotel staff and locals who have been in the area for a long time have also reported some strange experiences. They have heard sounds of dragging heavy goods on floors, sounds of throwing random stuff across rooms, and hysterical laughter and all of these made them feel utterly uneasy during their stay in the hotel. The hotel remained closed for a long period of time, showcasing the excuse of ongoing maintenance or repair but many believe that the actual reason was to find a remedy to the unexplainable haunting.

According to one story, the beginning of supernatural occurrences in the holiday home are all linked to the news of a young lady's suicide in its premises. The lady took her own life during her stay in a room in the hotel and since then, her unsatisfied soul wanders around the building, occasionally letting others know about her presence. Even exploring the sources around there did not lead to any further details about this occurrence. The news of unnatural death at any place brings a trail of uneasiness among others around the place.

The story of people hearing the sounds of dragging heavy furniture on the upper floor, despite there being no rooms on the floor above them, comes from the troop of actors and dancers from a popular Bollywood horror movie that was shot in this property. Reviewing the recorded camera rolls after the shooting, the editing team found an eerie sound coming from the camera audio, the sound of a young woman humming a song. Apart from this, the events like changing directions of the photos hanging on the walls in the hotel, the faucets in the washroom turning on automatically, not being able to reach the reception desk phone when needed, and a lot more of them are pretty famous. The fact that this hotel was closed for a long time has also made people think that something unnatural exists in this resort. When a place is known to be haunted, the people going there expect to experience something similar even before they set foot inside the door. Though psychologists explain this condition as anticipatory hallucination, popular belief of the masses overpowers any such scientific explanation.

This palatial construction of the hotel, built in an area covering about five-hundred acres of land in the lap of nature, stands as a haunted landmark, like the little black dot of evil among everything that's good in the symbol of Yang.

37

THE WELL IN THE OEL HOUSE

The city of Lucknow has a rich history. With the rhythm of Indian classical music, the air in Lucknow bears elements of hundreds of stories. The OEL House presents a gory chapter from history from the battle between the British and Nawab Wajid Ali Shah. Though this OEL House in the present day is the official residence of the Vice Chancellor of the Lucknow University, it has remained a haunted destination due to some occurrences in the past.

A common notion about Lucknow is that the city was established by the kings of Surya Dynasty. The reason shown behind the naming of this city is that when Lord Rama, Lady Sita, and Laxman returned to Ajodhya after their fourteen-year-long exile, Rama gifted this beautiful city, named Laxmanabati, to his brother Laxman. With time, the name Laxmanabati gradually morphed into Lucknow.

Another story tells us that the city was established by a person named Lakhna or Laxna and it was named Lucknow (pronounced Lakh-now) after him. The signature of aristocracy and tales from the past have remained here through establishments like the Bada Imambara, Chota Imambara, Rumi Darwaja, the mouth-watering savouries of Galawati Kebab, Tunde Kebab, the excellent production of Chikankari. The astonishing smell of attar, the floating tune of azan from the mosques and the music really keeps the air enchanted throughout the city.

While roaming around the well-known and famous places in Lucknow, if you ask your driver to stop by the OEL House, he would cross a broad road and stop in front of a big, white building. Standing in front of the large gate, you would instantly realize that the building has aged quite a bit, parts of it have been repaired as well. It won't come to the least of your suspicions that this very building had so many fearsome stories revolving around it. The beautifully decorated garden in the front lawn, the quarters of the employees, none of them let out any indication of the existence of anything unnatural. Knowing the structure of the house, and the context about it, you would feel like approaching it. Going through the broad way, there is a large door, various vehicles are always parked around it. The interior is covered with shadows and that are fairly prominent even during the day. A winding road leads to the backdoor of the house. There are many pretty flowering plants, most of which are ignored by people, and that is followed by a lawn that meets the wall that marks the end of the territory. There is a slight mound among the row of trees close to that wall. Near that, there is a covered well. There is a long history of this well, now covered for safety reasons. This is the source of so many horrific tales that surround this mansion.

The OEL house is presently the house of the Vice Chancellor of the University of Lucknow, but looking into the history of it we can find out that this very house once used to be a residence of Nawab Wajid Ali Shah. He was the last Nawab or the emperor of Awadh. He favoured creativity and patronized the flourishing artistic sides of his empire. The well in this compound has a story from the time of his rule. During the rebellion of 1857, a gruesome battle took place in this house between the British soldiers and the Indian revolutionaries. A countless number of British fighters were killed in that battle and thrown into this well. A popular belief suggests that the souls of those dead soldiers who never received a proper burial, roam around this well and this mansion to this day. Though this raised a lot of debates, the other strange fact is, there lies the dead body of a small child right beside this well. People believe that the child had to meet an untimely death because of the uncontented souls of the British soldiers staying in these premises. The child most probably playfully threw some stones into the well but the spirits, being enraged by the disturbance to their earthly bodies, killed the child for causing such an annoyance. Since the child's body was discovered near this well, the rumours about a supernatural presence in this area have grown stronger.

This well used to remain as it was until the incident with the child, it was sealed after that. There are several spooky tales about this place. Some people have heard strange noises coming from the under the cover of that well, and that noise seemed as if something was trying hard to get up and get out of the enclosure. An aura of horror surrounds the OEL house. Despite being in a pretty populated locality, and the well being sealed carefully, the curiosity among people about this mansion and the well has not declined even a bit. Even if we overlook the supernatural elements, in this historically eventful city of Lucknow that has witnessed so many royal families and their countless little incidents, this OEL house has remained a remarkable landmark. The tale about the wails and screams of dead soldiers trying to get out of the death pit has been circulating among the masses for ages. Once the well was sealed, people began to hope that an incident as sad as the death of that little child would not recur in the future. Maybe the history that got covered under the lid of the water-well, would be lost over time, or maybe someday, someone would uncover a strange new future by taking that lid off. We can only wait to witness which course the time takes.

38

THE ABANDONMENT OF KULDHARA

People who had to abandon their ancestral residence and belongings to move to someplace new are spread across the globe. People have always had to leave their homes, their motherlands, to face the unknown, carrying only the memory of what life used to be for them. Those who are forced to move due to wars, and political unrests, carry a sad story about their beautiful life before those incidents. Alongside these sad stories, there are also accounts of adjusting to the new life, hustling to make ends meet, and creating their own communities. What if instead of changing, the places they left were abandoned forever? What if no one else could successfully settle down at those places? What if they were haunted by something nobody ever expected to exist? It is not just about a house, not even a fixed place. What if, the supernatural entities get a hold of an entire village that was once full of life? What if people from faraway places come to visit this village just to observe how devastated it is? Kuldhara is such a village in the Jaisalmer district of Rajasthan, vacated by humans and ruled by the unnatural. Kuldhara remains the same to this day, a village with a strange story and many unanswered questions.

This village, located near the boundaries of the Thar desert, has stopped in time with the ruins of houses, roads, and temples. There are mentions of Kuldhara in the ancient book *Tarikh-e-Jaisalmer* by Laxmi Chand. From this book, we come to know that the first civilization started in this place with a Paliwal Brahmin who went by the name of Karhan. There has been a great amount of research on the history of Kuldhara. Studying the stone tablets, it was discovered that Kuldhara was the name of a lineage or a tribe among the Paliwal Brahmins. The village was named after the tribe of people who lived here. Once upon a time a lot of surrounding villages were built along with Kuldhara. Tracing the stories circulated among the local people, there is no specific discrepancy around how the village was established but quite a few variations can be found amid the tales about how the civilization came to an end in this village. The rumour suggests that the entire population of this village suddenly vanished on the day of Rakhi Purnima in the year 1825. Since then, not a single person has lived here. Rows of mud houses are now falling vacant. Despite the existence of several other villages surrounding Kuldhara, this one place remained uninhabited for ages. But what exactly caused this absurdity?

The refugees carry a painful history with them, with the passing of time the tales that gathered and added up with the rumours around this village has a mention of a powerful man from that time. It is thought that the demise of this village was largely influenced by the-then ruler of the Jaisalmer constituency, Salim Singh. When the Paliwal Brahmins were still residing in this village located eighteen kilometres away from Jaisalmer, the ruler Salim Singh felt an attraction towards the daughter of the head of this village. Salim was determined to marry that girl. Neither the family of the village-head, nor the main advisors of the village agreed to lend Salim the hand of the head's daughter. Denied from fulfilling his lust, Salim took off his mask of decency and revealed the fangs of power. He threatened to harm the safety of the villagers if they opposed the marriage. The advisors of Kuldhara and surrounding villages held a meeting, and upon discussion, they chose to vacate the village entirely instead of submitting to such an unethical urge. Leaving your home is not an easy thing to do and people face a lot of emotions when they are forced to do so. These Brahmins, when leaving, let out a curse on the villages so that nobody can move in and stay in these premises after them. It is doubtful whether curses work at all or not, but really, nobody could build a residence in this village for centuries since that incident in 1825. People did try to build colonies around this place many times. But whenever someone tried to make this almost well-equipped village their home, some kind of mishap took place with them or their families. These families faced deaths, entire changes in the behaviour of family members, violence within the family, and a lot more as soon as they tried to live in Kuldhara. A few rumours state that some immigrants lost their abilities to speak as they saw something really terrifying in this village. Whatever the reason, a community could never be formed in Kuldhara for nearly a couple of centuries now. The government of Rajasthan has declared this abandoned village as a tourist attraction.

According to the statistics from the writings of a British officer named James Todd, even in 1815, about two thousand people used to live in Kuldhara. And now the entire landscape is a lifeless land with ruins of roads, temples, and houses that once used to be homes for some people. People have tried several times to explain the migration of people from the village. They put the blame on the rough desert weather and lack of rain at that time. But the fact that the entire village population disappeared without an announcement, within the span of a day, still remains unexplainable by reasoning. There are also stories about other, probably supernatural, incidents that occur here to this day. There were some people who tried walking by the roads after the sunset but they kept forgetting the routes and their sense of direction was numbed. The temperature in the ruins of this village falls drastically in the evening. Wailing, sobbing, and screams for help can be heard from this place around the middle of the night.

A lot of people who believe in the existence of ghosts or the life after death of the mortal body, think that the unhappy spirits of the people who were forced to move out of Kuldhara at that time, still roam around the landscape at night, trying to live in their beloved motherland. The way their curses have kept people from settling down in the lands of Kuldhara, the same way, they themselves are continuing to live here as the spirits.

While roaming the popular places in Rajasthan and feasting on the beauty of this gorgeous state, you can take out a little time to have a short trip to this abandoned, and almost forgotten village that remained still at a point in history. A village, where there used to be laughter, children playing around, the noise of markets, people going to work but now it is only some remains of mud houses and temples and the roads. Maybe, while gazing at the ruins of Kuldhara and remembering the story you just read, a faint cry from the past would end up reaching your ears. Maybe you would be the one to uncover the mystery of Kuldhara and get to know a story that no one else has heard.

39

THE INVISIBLE GUARD AT THE FARRUKHNAGAR FORT

In the year of 1732, Faujdar Khan had built the Farrukhnagar fort. This fort was planned and built according to the ideal Mughal construction style, making it a great attraction for tourists travelling from all over the country. Farrukhnagar is a city located within the premises of Gurgaon, in the state of Haryana. This town shares its boundary with the district of Jhajjar and geographically, its position is in the Ahirwal region. The region of Ahirwal was developed around the Rewari town and during the Mughal regime, it was ruled by the Ahiri descendants. This town too, was established by Faujdar Khan for the purpose of participating in the lucrative trade of salt that was manufactured from the saline water which could be collected from the wells of a dozen villages located around this town. After the Mughals, it was ruled by the Jatts, followed by the British. The city has seen the regimes of various rulers from a variety of backgrounds and cultures. Surrounding the Farrukhnagar fort, there remains a long-standing belief among the locals. They claim the fort is protected by one security guard who is not a human being, but a spirit. The strange existence of an undetectable being has remained around this fort from the day it was built to the time when it began nearing its ruins. Located close to the Sultanpur Bird Sanctuary, this fort is safe to the visitors who are following the rules to enter the premises, but the fort has brought deadly fates to those who have trespassed or entered it without abiding by the rules.

The construction of the fort occurred nearly three centuries ago, but the tale of an invisible guard has permanently stuck with it since. When the fort was inaugurated, it had the capacity to host four thousand people. The local people also called it the Dilli Darwaja. When the site was close to being in complete ruins, initiatives were taken for reconstructing it and because of that much of its former glory has been restored. As time passed people have told and retold the story to each other, and layers of exaggeration have coated the actual event. During the construction work, when the workers needed to gather supplies in one place by carrying them from long distances, they felt so tired that they could not even perform the bare necessities at the time of requirements. On one such a hot summer day, the exhausted workers saw a stranger had brought water for them. They had never seen that man in the locality before. He brought cold water for everyone till their thirst was quenched and then walked away without saying a word more. Drinking that water, the workers felt a gust of enthusiasm for their work and they magically began feeling much better. The pending work for that day was completed pretty fast. Those workers searched for the man a lot after that day to thank him, but none of them could find any sign of him.

Another story is from a much later time. This incident does not directly involve the locals but they were involved in the after effects and the reaction to the incident. One morning, a man was spotted unconscious right beside the fort. People rushed in as soon as he was spotted and started to help him, but the man was not in a condition to even open his eyelids. After treating him with care, the curious crowd began asking how he ended up in a situation like that. The man said that he had heard about hidden treasures located inside the fort and he trespassed in the darkness of the night. As soon as he breached the property and began wandering around, he felt like someone was following him. No matter which way he walked in, someone kept following his each and every step. Being creeped out, he decided to take out the threat. He stopped, turned around, and swung the crowbar he was holding in the direction where he sensed his follower to be. His crowbar was stuck mid-air, but he could not see anybody behind him. The guy realized that he was being followed by an invisible person and he stopped the attack. The invisible follower was holding the crowbar with a formidable strength. He tried with all his might but could not release his weapon in any way, he was no match to his opponent in terms of sheer physical strength. While standing in shock, his body was suddenly flung away, as if someone kicked him very hard. Then he felt like being choked by a person standing on his chest and grabbing his throat. He was being forced down on the floor, and all his attempts at getting up were going in vain. That unstoppable force now approached his eyes, two thumbs began pressing his eye sockets. After experiencing that tremendous amount of pain, he gathered whatever was left of his strength and tried to stand up. As soon as he began lifting his body from the ground, another such heavy kick fell on his chest. His painful scream tore apart the silence of the Farrukhnagar fort in the middle of the dark night. But there was not a single human within the bounds of the fort to hear his scream. His body did not have enough strength left to regain its balance after that kick. He fell from there to the ground outside the fort and lost consciousness. When he regained his senses, he tried opening his eyes and found out that he was not able to see anything. All that he stared at was nothing but darkness. Entering the fort at night, greedy for the hidden treasure cost him dearly.

The people who visit this fort during the hours scheduled by the governing authority have never reported any unusual experiences. Neither has any new story spawned from this place in a very long time. But those people who come here at various times, motivated by money and stories of hidden treasure have met with one or the other kind of ill fate. Beginning from the person who came to supply potable water to the tired laborers during the construction of the fort, people believe in an invisible power that is the mighty protector of the fort. This historical monument, constructed centuries ago, hosts a supernatural entity within its boundaries. A power that can turn someone blind and kick them out from the premises of the fort if that person enters the gate with any ill intentions. The existence of the invisible guard has been reported from the time it was built, and the beliefs about it have not weakened even after the original buildings of the fort were close to ruins. And that power has its own conscience and judgmental abilities that allow it to reveal its existence and punish only those with bad intentions.

40

THE GRAVEYARD OF KALPALLI

'That's the kind of thought you have when you're not in your senses.'

'I told you! You don't have to believe anything I am saying. But trust me, I am telling the truth, just the way I saw it. I don't plan on making everyone believe this story anyway.' Sumit angrily replied to Palash.

They are a small group of four friends, Sumit, Palash, Prakash, and Bijoy. After a long time, they finally got a chance to meet up. They used to be colleagues in their first job in Bangalore. Sumit had stayed back there and got an apartment for himself. Sumit's wife had taken the kids to her father's place and the apartment was empty for a few days. Being bored alone, passing days like he used to as a bachelor in the city, he called up some old friends here. The topic of today's discussion was ghosts. They were sharing spooky stories, someone pulled up a story that they had heard as children when visiting their grandpa's place, someone talked about the supernatural entities they have heard about roaming around their office spaces...the atmosphere was getting a bit heavy with all those scary elements. This apartment was in a high rise. They could see the lights from distant buildings, the windows of other high-rise constructions lit up in a strange pattern. The clock was way past midnight, a cold breeze was coming through the windows. It has the perfect ambience for horror stories. After listening to the stories that everyone had heard from someone else or read somewhere, Sumit spoke of his own recent experience. The atmosphere changed after that story. None of the others had any experience of their own, but Sumit's tale was quite intimidating. Palash was not ready to believe any of that, he waived off all the possibilities of it being anywhere close to reality.

It took about twenty minutes to reach the office on the bike from Sumit's house. Bangalore is famous for being an IT centre. Sumit had been staying there for quite a few years now. He had been around many places within the city as well as the outskirts. Then he had heard of some supernatural incidents at a place, close to where he lived. Listening to the story from the maid servant of his household, he did not want to believe it the first time and now, when he shared his experience with his friends, nobody believed him this time either.

The place was St. John's Cemetery. After coming to know about the name of the place from the maid, he looked it up on Google, and there were quite a few links with information about it. The incident started strangely. Things were going missing very frequently from his apartment and Sumit jokingly stated that some ghost was messing around with them. From that they were talking about many spooky incidents around the town and eventually landed on the story of the Kalpalli graveyard. Sumit was a bit irked by seeing how many people talk about a place like this. Even in today's modern era.

It is an old graveyard by the Old Madras Road and loads of scary, eerie stories have formed around it. More than a few people would refuse to travel along that road during the night. Some have also seen something unnatural there. Stories of supernatural entities are not uncommon around graveyards or crematoriums. Tales from the notion of death and the probable presence of souls that could not leave the earth after their bodies were no longer alive, but Kalpalli graveyard is one of the most popular places like that.

Sumit's logical mind made out that probably a group of goons are behind the rumours to keep nosey people from interfering in their illegal business and they are probably making the graveyard one of their bases. But as time passed, Sumit's curiosity about that place was eventually vanquished. A few months passed. Life was going on the way it should. Mundane, routine, peaceful. Sumit was busy with his corporate life and the adorable family that he had. Suddenly one day, he came across a news story on his Facebook feed that said a team of ghost hunters came to visit this graveyard and two of their members fell severely sick after returning from the place. The name of Kalpalli lit a spark in Sumit's mind. His curiosity began boiling once again. What was exactly happening in that graveyard?

That day he was finished with his office a little earlier. Usually, he needs to stay back till eight o'clock in the evening but that day he was done before that. He hadn't been out roaming alone on his bike for a long time. Just commuting between the office and the apartment, and if he goes out during the weekends, it is always with the family. That day was his chance to give it a go, and enjoy some alone time on his bike before going back home. Kalpalli graveyard and the address of Old Madras Road struck his mind. Would it be okay to go to a place like that alone? He hesitantly started in that direction. As he kept progressing, the localities gradually started becoming less dense. Google Maps showed him only 4 minutes left to reach the destination.

This area had a lot of trees and the street lamps were a bit dim. Were all those stories about this place true? People would be easily scared in an empty place like that if they were left there alone in the evening. He could hear the distant barking of a dog. He parked his bike, locked the handle, and walked towards the front of the graveyard. Not a single person was in the vicinity and so many people were buried within the enclosure, staying there for decades. A lot of ghost-sighting stories had emerged from this place.

Sumit pulled out a cigarette and sparked his lighter to light it up. The attempts were futile, the lighter would not light anyway. An irritated Sumit walked back to his bike and thought of leaving the place. He suddenly spotted that a strange man was gazing at him. The man was not even blinking. He had a creepy, empty stare. Sumit was a bit startled at first, but then he came back to his senses. To lighten up the tense situation, he asked the man if he had a lighter or some matches or not. There was no response from the man. Sumit let out a nervous smile and proceeded to unlock his bike. But lo! The key was not cooperating either. He tried a few times but all in vain, the bike would not release the lock. A chill ran down his spine, what was this eerie feeling? He looked back at that man, he was still there, still with the same empty gaze, his eyes unblinking.

Sumit began feeling a little scared, he felt sweat on his back, forehead, and palms. He decided to try to walk his bike away from this creep, it would be at least a little bit relieving if he could manage to get away from there. Sumit could not do that either. He understood that his legs were frozen by some strong force. Anxiety kicked in. Sumit's limbs began shaking mildly. He pulled out his phone from his pocket and tried to dial a friend. The phone was out of network coverage. Every second started to feel like an hour.

After God knows how much time passed, Sumit could hear a car horn. Someone was coming his way. The sound of a car engine followed shortly. Sumit looked back at that strange guy staring at him. He had vanished! The car headlamps lit up the road. Sumit saw it was the patrolling car of the local police department. He was stuttering so much that he could not explain anything to the policeman. Rather, the police rebuked him for standing alone in a place like this at night, and also advised him to get away. This time the bike unlocked in one attempt and the engine roared as soon as he pressed the button.

Sumit never visited that place again, but that memory of the blank stare from the creepy man haunts him frequently when he travels alone in the evening. No human being can have that kind of gaze and no one alive could stare for so long without blinking even once. Palash decided to visit the graveyard after listening to the story. Sumit knew from the bottom of his heart that even if every single one of his friends decided to visit that place, he would not resist but he himself would not set foot near that graveyard at any cost.

ACKNOWLEDGEMENTS

I would like to thank the journalists, doctors, police officers, and numerous locals who assisted my research for this book. Thanks also to Chunilal Banerjee and Anandarup Chakraborty. I am grateful to Raka and all my family members, teachers, and friends.